Printed and published by:
BoD - Books on Demand, Norderstedt
ISBN: 9-783-751905-244
Copyright: Dr. Klaus Biedermann
Photographs: Dr. Klaus Biedermann
Cover design by Eva Lindorf
Translation: Christine Yuill

A Year and a Day Ago

NOVEL

Klaus Biedermann

Third edition

Dedicated to my grandmother, Helene

'

'We are souls. The soul is not ruled by space and time.
The soul is infinite.' (Ram Dass)

"I inhale the sweet breath that leaves your mouth. I see your loveliness every day.

It is my desire to hear your soft voice like the breath of the north wind, that my bones may be rejuvenated by my love for you.

Give me your hands that hold your spirit, that I may receive it and live through him.

Call me by my name until the end of eternity and I shall want for nothing."

(belated anonymous inscription in the gold-plated Ikhnaton sarcophagus)

The science of soul mates is an unspoken truth, an adventure broaching the sharing of feelings with another, who is really oneself. The more open, aware you are with your feelings, the more conscious your partner is about them because you are permeable to this knowledge. This permeability, this process can happen in this place, irrespective of where the partner of your being is, because it takes place on a conscious level. Your feel the emotions of it, and you realise it. Do you understand? (Ramtha)

Similarities with living people are not coincidental,
with the exception of Sophie and Rolf.

————————————

My thanks go out to the Mouzakitis family for their
generous hospitality, to my friend Konstantinos Louv-
ros for his enduring assistance; to Petra Huber and
Klaus Wohlleb for their loving management of the
Ouranos Club; Dimitris Kourkulos for his inside
knowledge and to my old school-friend Albert Lem-
bach who shuffled all the commas into place.

My special thanks go out to
Dimitria Gemitzoglou, Elanor and
Christine Yuill, who translated this book into Greek
and English, respectively.

— — — — — — — — —

Foreword

The romance between soul mates has captured the fantasy of mankind since the dawn of ages - that somewhere out there, there is a magical 'someone,' who will fill the emptiness and make us happy: the perfect counterpart.

We almost always believe to have found this person when we fall in love.

Then we talk of the infamous "same wavelength" and "complete familiarity" so much so, that it seems that "one feels as though they have known each other for an eternity," etc. etc..

I presume, my dear reader, that you yourself have also experienced this. Yes, I hope you have. But what can happen is that after a certain amount of time, you notice that you are no longer on the same "infamous" wavelength and that the other person (it is always the other) has changed.

This, however, is not correct, the other person hasn't changed, they just don't fulfil your expectations anymore. Then you are disappointed.

You are the one who fell for a deception. The other person has not changed, your image of him, or her, that you had illustrated in such vibrant colours, is no longer the same. If the partner then leaves you, then the whole house of cards falls apart.

Love is unconditional, love is accepting. If this acceptance does not originate from you, there is no chance of you ever being able to accept anybody else.

CHAPTER 1

Did you know your path can wind itself over hills and through valleys and gorges, passing dreamy plains? Away beyond rivers and oceans and babbling brooks? Did you know it can lead under the sea, and over the ocean? How will you ever know whether you're on the right path? If you wear a smile on your face; if what you do makes you feel happy and fills you with joy. The right path will always be where you are happy. (Ramtha)

Saturday

From the skies, usually mild, yet sometimes overcast, but always dutifully watching over the shady olive groves and merging into the blue of the sea somewhere in the distance, Dr. Sophie Leiter arrived in Corfu for the first time ever in her life.

In Germany, everything had settled neatly into place. She loved her job as a doctor in a hospital in Muenster, here she had found her true vocation. After a few disappointments, Michael walked into her life and Sophie knew he'd be the one she wanted to grow old with. At the moment, they were in a long-distance relationship, but Sophie was happy. Everything was turning out for the best.

At the airport, Rolf was waiting in the small café that was at the end of the street in front of the departure hall. He'd already spotted her, as she was standing on the pavement with her suitcase, searching. Crowds of tourists were streaming out of the building, heading in the direction of the many buses and taxis which were to transfer them to their holiday resorts.

He'd promised his friend, Martha, to pick Sophie up from the airport, and she had given him a photo of her to take with him.

"So that you recognise Sophie. And don't you dare come back without her!" she'd said, laughing. A few years ago, the two women had worked together in the hospital and they had become friends. Since then, Martha had married a Greek man, with whom she managed a small guest house in the north-west of the Island.

Sophie was wearing jeans, a light blue sweatshirt and red trainers. She couldn't wait to discover how Martha had adapted to her completely new life. During the flight, she had remembered the send-off in the hospital and the heart-warming words of the senior consultant, Prof. Dr. Boek.

'Doctor Werner, when you go, this hospital will be losing an outstanding doctor and I deeply regret you are leaving. However, everyone here can understand that you're just following the calling of your heart. That is what makes an excellent cardiologist, after all! I'd therefore like to present this parting gift from all of us to you, with our heartfelt thanks.'

Martha had been moved to tears as she unpacked the life-sized porcelain heart decorated in the Greek national colours.

2

Rolf stood up and threw the paper cup from which he'd been drinking a frappé into a dustbin.

"You must be Sophie. I'm Rolf, welcome to Corfu! Martha wanted to come herself, but her little daughter isn't very well today, so she decided to stay home instead."

He showed her the photo.

"Martha sent me a message with a photo of you just before my take off to make sure I wouldn't drive away with some other man," Sophie said, laughing and brushing one of her brown curls behind her ear, "I hope it's nothing too serious with the little one?"

"No, I don't think so, it's something to do with her stomach. She went to a children's birthday party yesterday ... I won't say any more. Is this your first visit to Corfu?"

"Even to Greece at all, actually." She smiled. "But Martha was so enraptured by it every time she came that I just had to come here once to see. Good thing you speak my language, I don't speak any Greek except for the two words *Iassu* and *Kalimera*. Where did you learn to speak German so well?"

"At home," Rolf laughed, "I'm from Bonn. About thirty years ago I came here for the first time with my parents. Then shortly after finishing school with a friend in an old Renault 4, then later a couple more times. Three years ago, I finally decided to move here entirely."

"Oh, I used to have a car like that too, dashboard gear stick!" she simulated the gear change movement with her hand.

"Yes, you're right, a good car. All the camping gear would fit into it easily. Incidentally, a lot of people initially take me for a Greek."

They loaded Sophie's suitcase and hand luggage into his small Suzuki Jeep and set off.

"I can close the top if you like. It tends to get a little chilly later in the mountains."

"No, this is wonderful! I have brought something suitable with me, please leave it open, then we can see better too."

Sophie pulled out a scarf out of her bag.

Exactly the colour of her hair, he thought.

"Martha already told me it would probably be a good idea to pack some warm things, too."

"That definitely makes sense for the evenings in May. I've just got to pick up something in a shop in Dassia, it won't take long. We'll reach Arillas in about an hour."

"No problem, I'm on holiday."

Suddenly, his mobile rang.

"It was Martha, she wanted to know if you arrived safely. You seem to have your phone switched off."

"She's right, it's still on inflight mode." Sophie remembered.

"She told me it would be a good idea to go and drink a coffee somewhere, she wants to finish your apartment first. She hasn't been able to do it until now because of Maria. Well, if that is okay with you, of course."

"Yes, it sure is. How's the little one?"

"She seems to be a bit better now, she had a stomach upset, just as I thought."

He'd lost count of how often Sophie had expressed her excitement during their drive to the north-west part of the island.

They were driving through a sea of blossoms, made up of broom and dark red poppies, amid gnarled olive groves, bushes of orange Lantana flowers, huge oleander bushes and meadows full of midday flowers. The air was filled with the sweet scent of the surrounding flora.

"What a wonderful sight!" Sophie exclaimed excitedly.

"Yes, they even flower here until September because the wind brings enough moisture from the Albanian mountains and the Greek mainland and now and again it rains too."

This island, which Rolf could recognize purely by its scent, he had long since considered his home.

After a short stop in *Dassia* they drove into *Dafni* for a short break.

Sophie stepped onto the terrace of the café Melisito and gazed at the rolling countryside. She did so with such an intensity, that it made Rolf sense that this was far more than just the simple amazement of a tourist who was visiting Corfu for their first time. This magical island, this crescent of land in the Ionic sea, that had been fought over so often and had already captivated many kings and queens, also now moved her deeply.

Her gaze wandered over the wide green valley to the gently rolling hills where proud cypress trees stood to attention, like silent watchmen amidst the olive groves, ready to confront the slightest foe. Small villages clung on to the steep hillsides, which disappeared at some point into the sea only to rise out again, wilder and steeper, merging with the Albanian mountains.

Smiling, she turned to him, her brown eyes shining.

"It is so beautiful here!"

"I'm glad it pleases you."

"Pleases me? ... it is far more than *pleasing* ... it is simply fantastic! I can understand Martha already *now*."

"How long will you be staying?"

"Two weeks, no, fifteen days even! I can hardly believe that I am allowing myself so long."

"Oh, then you will still be here for the name-day of Martha's husband and his cousin Helena. It's even more important than birthdays here in Greece. It means a big party."

"I have never eaten such a delicious piece of lemon cake, it's just the right combination of meringue and lemon. Not too sweet, not too sour. I bet the lemons are from the trees growing over there." said Sophie over a cappuccino and cake during their stop.

"Maybe they are, the apple pie is very good too though."

"I wasn't planning on fattening myself up too much." Sophie laughed.

"Maybe you could come by here again during your stay, it's not far from your apartment."

"Well I'll almost definitely do that ... if only for the view: Shall we not say 'Du' to each other? We are both friends of Martha, after all."

"Yes, that'd be fine with me, Sophie. That's generally how it is. Anyway, on the whole they are fairly relaxed here, if you maintain Greek habits, that is. One shouldn't overdo it with them though."

"No, of course not! I'd better ask Martha to explain the ins and outs of Greek etiquette to me."

He glanced at his mobile.

"We can set off now, your room is ready. Martha is looking forward to your arrival, it isn't far now, only a couple of kilometres."

"Then let's go, I can't wait to see her again, she has just written to me too. Let me get the tab, if you don't mind, you have picked me up from the airport after all!"

"Thank you very much, I accept!"

"My word, it is quite rough here," said Sophie sometime later, "Now I know why you drive a Jeep ... the state of these roads!"

"Yes, it is really the most suitable vehicle for Corfu." he laughed.

CHAPTER 2

The thing is that life should not consist of a process of searching; it is an admissible gift. To wander around, searching for someone who fills the gaps, to search for someone who makes your day brighter, that's not the solution. If you can't watch the sunrise or dance alone under the starlit sky like an elf, someone else at your side won't make it better either. Do you understand that? (Ramtha)

As they drove up the driveway, they could see the small family standing at the front door. Martha was holding her daughter and waving excitedly.

"I'm so glad to see her again, Rolf. Five years is such a long time!" Sophie exclaimed happily.

A statement she was going to change her mind about a few days later.

"Sophie!", called Martha, "It's wonderful that you managed to make it! I'm so happy! How long has it been since we last saw each other? May I introduce you to my husband Kostas and our daughter Maria?"

Well, that's the perfect man for Martha, and Maria takes just after her Mother, Sophie thought at once, after Kostas also hugged her with a laugh.

"Welcome to my home, Sophie! Martha has already told me lots about you... It's nice that you are here. You can't imagine how happy you have made my wife ... Oh, and me too, of course!"

"Thanks very much! So, you speak German too, that's

very convenient for me. Shall we not say 'Du' to each other? It would be a bit strange if I only say 'Du' to Martha."

"But of course! I worked at ThyssenKrupp in Duisburg for ten years, that's why. After that, I built the guest house on my grandparent's land... Then Martha decided to walk into my life, like a beautiful colourful butterfly."

"When she visited a seminar here, right? That's what she told me."

Martha laughed: "Yes Sophie, that was the best seminar of my entire life! I skived off the last two days of it though."

"Let me guess why."

"Nope, no need! He's standing here in front of you. Wait a second I'll get the key to the apartment and take you over."

After Rolf had taken Sophie's luggage from the car and brought it into her room, he looked around the apartment that Martha had just shown her friend proudly. It was part of a bungalow, painted a pale shade of yellow with four separate entrances. There was a tastefully furnished living space with a small adjoining kitchen, a bathroom with a shower and a bedroom with a large double bed.

"So, I'll leave you in peace to unpack," said Martha, "And pick you up later … or just come on over when you are ready."

He had never been inside the guest house before, previously he had just visited their private house which was located a little bit further up the olive grove.

"You have a very nice apartment here, Sophie. The other ones will probably all be occupied soon too. The seminar season has already begun, you know. Martha and Kostas let rooms to the guests of the Ouranos club."

"Yes, she told me that already. I probably won't be here much anyway though, I'll be lying on the beach all day, sunning myself or exploring the island with Martha!" Sophie laughed. "I'll just jump in the shower and get changed. You can go over already if you like, I'll join you later."

He stepped through the open door of the living room onto the patio. The house was built at the edge of the olive grove and through the leaves of the trees it was possible to see the sea and a small island. The sunlight gave the leaves of the olive trees a silver shimmer in the gentle breeze. Suddenly, his vision went blurred ... his eyes closed and then images appeared in his mind.

„Nikos, hurry up! These olives must be in Kassiopi by this afternoon! Bring them to the press right away and no wasting time at the harbour again, do you hear me?"

His father helped him to tie the heavy sacks full of black fruit onto the back of the donkey. Nikos pities the poor animal, even though he knows how strong it is. A cold mist ascends from the valley and he shivers. But in the plain, it'll be warmer in the April sun.

He has spent the last few weeks picking the olives with his mother. They don't have many trees and they have had to give a part of the crops to the rich landowner, Angelos Pachos, just like all the other farmers in the region. He knows that the biggest part of the landowner's wealth comes from Venice. Ten gold coins had been given to every one of them who planted a hundred trees... And Angelos Pachos owns a lot of land.

During harvest-time he isn't allowed to visit the monastery on the peak of the Pantokrator and the school is closed - the only two things he loves.

He bends down to his young dog, strokes and pets him. "Kleitos, one day, we'll be rich, won't we? And then you'll sleep in a silk bed, I promise you!"

Kleitos is his whole pride and best friend, next to Spiros, of course, with whom he goes to school with. The love for books and scripts of the great Homer connects the two. They are the only two at school who can read well. Something his father calls worthless. What they can't learn in school, they are taught by the monk Angelos in Ypsilos, Pantokratoras. He told them how the monastery had been built in the middle of the

11

fifth century as a colonial settlement.

The ascetic Artemios Paisos, has been sculptured from stone up there, it is said that he may even have made it himself. Angelos patiently spends a lot of hours with the two friends during which they read the bible and other old scripts. During this time, the desire to become a priest had emerged in his mind, but this is his big secret. Of course, his father has other plans for him. Soon, he will be thirteen and therefore old enough to watch over the sheep of the village. Extra money that the family needs desperately. He knows that. In four months, there will be another fair up on the mountain and many people from his and other villages will be there. Maybe he will get the chance to speak with Helena again. Sometimes, she smiles at him in school. Spiros laughed at him some time ago. "You always blush when she looks at you. Is it possible you might have fallen for her?"

But that, of course, is nonsense, because she's the daughter of the richest man around and he himself is one of the poorest here.

"So, time to get going," his father says, pulling him out of his daydream. "And be sure you're home by nightfall. You know how your mother worries."

The oil warehouse is a low stone building with a floor that consists of compressed earth. He isn't the only one delivering the valuable wares here. Women wearing brightly coloured clothes and carrying baskets are standing in long rows, waiting for their olives to be weighed. The stone bunkers are slowly filling. Two donkeys are tied to a big millstone which they will be moving for hours. But he has no time to watch any longer. After his olives are weighed, an ancient, grim looking man hands him a dirty piece of paper. With great care he puts away the valuable receipt into the pocket of his trousers that doesn't already have a hole in it. He leads his donkey away, past the wooden press in which the men will stack the greyish- black mass later. He still remembers that from the year before, when he'd come here for the first time without his father.

The memory of the beating he had earned for coming home late last time was still very clear in his mind and because he wanted to make a detour via the harbour on the way back, he started to hurry. He loved watching the great sailing ships laden with huge barrels full of the valuable oil, which now departed daily. It was with this oil, that the streets of Venice would be lit up. One day, he promised to himself once more, he would see this sight with his own eyes.

It is already late afternoon, when he passes the last houses of the town, which clearly mirror the poverty of the inhabitants. He swings himself up onto the donkey and urges him on. Dogs chase after them, barking loudly.

Rolf was torn out of his daydream by a dog barking nearby. In the meantime, Sophie had already unpacked her things and had joined him on the terrace.

"Are you feeling okay?", she asked, concerned.

He slowly turned around to her.

"Yes, I'm ... I´m fine, thanks."

Where on earth was he just now? Sophie asked herself, *he seemed miles away.*

"Sophie, where were you?" Martha approached her, laughing. The two friends embraced.

"We're waiting for you with the coffee and cake and my parents-in-law are desperate to meet you. They've invited us over to have dinner with them later. You see, your first day is already booked up!"

"Oh, we've just had some cake, but because it's you, I'm sure I'll manage a second piece, too. I can't promise I'll be able to eat anything this evening, though."

"You just wait, you will be hungry later. In Greece you usually have dinner quite late. Rolf, you're invited too, I still owe you that taxi fare. Thanks again for picking Sophie up for me."

"That's very kind of you, Martha, but I still have a lot to do at home and you two probably have loads to catch up on" and turning to Sophie, he said, "we'll probably meet again fairly soon, this place isn't that big. Arillas beach is beautiful and the water temperature is already quite inviting. In the afternoon I'm often at the Ammos Beach Bar. It's right on the beach... if you'd like to have a coffee with me sometime."

"Sure, but I'd like to get to know the island as well as I can in these fourteen days, as well."

"Rolf is the best tour guide I know, he probably has seen more of this island than Kostas, and he was born here. Right, Rolf?" Martha laughed.

"I guess you're right. Well, at least regarding the northern side of the island. I don't get around the southern part very much, even though there are so many magical beaches with proper dunes and high waves there. But it's a lot of driving and I find there are too many tourists around there during the high season."

"Well, I'd be glad to accept your offer seeing as though you seem to be in charge of Rolf's free time!" Sophie smiled and winked cheekily at Martha.

"Oh, I'm so sorry, Rolf", Martha apologised. "I didn't want to impose on you. But why don't you come over afterwards, we have enough for everyone. You know how much mother likes to dish up!"

"Thanks a lot for the invitation, Martha, but I'm afraid I've already made plans ... And I really don't mind taking over the role of tourist guide, I have plenty of time at the moment. But I really must be getting on, though. Goodbye, you two!"

CHAPTER 3

There are some among you, who are terribly unhappy. I can see it in you. Well, I have no pity for you, because through a far wider reaching understanding I have realised you planned it so, you wanted it so. You want to feel the way you feel. Things will only be different if you want them to change. Nothing, no-one, no power in the entire universe will be able to change your stubborn attitude. You see, the key to the door of understanding is on your side of the door. You are a God, and whatever you desire for your kingdom, so be it! This single, sublime law, can never be disputed or overturned. Do you understand? (Ramtha)

Originally, Arillas had been a typical fishing village but it had been growing rapidly over the past few decades. When Rolf visited the place the first time with his parents, there had only been a hotel and two taverns. The *Graziella* at the end of the beach with its friendly head chef Thomaso Bardis and his sons, Kostas and Aristides, who are still managing the place today. The second tavern on the edge of town was called the *Gravia*, named after a small offshore island. Nowadays it is called Brouklis and is well worth a visit. In the past, you still had a panoramic view of the sea from there.

Dimitris, the son of the former owner Spiros Kourkulos, had at some point renamed the tavern after his grandfather, Brouklis. That was the name that Greek people seeking their fortune in Brooklyn used to be called. Aside of his work as a restaurant proprietor, Dimitri was involved in environmental protection and had already achieved a lot for community of Arillas.

No matter where a guest comes from, they would be invariably greeted in their native language. In addition, they served tasty dishes with short anecdotes from the life in Arillas on the side.

These days, there wasn't a single full-time fisherman left in Arillas. Instead, you can find various cafés, three hotels, a boat hire, a hairdresser, car leases and travel agencies, mini markets and souvenir shops all waiting for customers. While strolling through the narrow alleys there are plenty of different languages to be heard. The vast majority of the inhabitants live off tourism in summer and on agriculture and fishing in the winter. Since the tourism is limited to private guest houses and family-run hotels, Arillas is considered a popular destination for those who travelled individually. A remarkable feature is the very warm and friendly atmosphere, although this applies to the whole of the island of Corfu.

Arillas is considered to be the *spiritual centre* of Corfu. There are numerous seminar centres that offer many diverse programs with international spiritual leaders available from May until October. There is something for everyone on offer.

Highlights are the certainly the old established Ouranos Club and Alexis Zorbas. Mythos arrived a few years ago, it is run by Gerda and Jochen, two German nationals who have already been living on the island for a long time.

You don't have to book a seminar right away. At the Ouranos Club it is possible to take part in the offered programme without obligation. Included are drawing- and sculpture courses in the olive grove under the guidance of Dimitra Klironomou, yoga courses or mantra singing, book lectures, dancing nights, family constellations and a lot more, including wonderfully and lovingly prepared meals straight from the organic vegetarian kitchen.

During the past few years, the Greeks have observed a phenomenon that doesn't meeting with the approval of all the inhabitants. There seems to be at least one new "spiritual" club springing up out of the ground every year. These new centres don't even sport Greek names (like for example the Ouranos, the Alexis and the Mythos), but instead outlandish ones, such as 'Dharma' 'Gayatri' or 'Buddhahall.' The proprietors and their guests, dress themselves in traditional Indian clothes, build statues of Buddha, and advertise with the most varied forms of meditation that are then practised on the beach or other public places. They organize events with titles such as "Sound- and Silence-Festival," "Embody Dance & Yoga" or "Silent Music Retreat" which at first only used to last for a few days, but now often extend over a several weeks! As the participants of these activities often make advanced reservations for their accommodation, this causes lasting effects on the traditional tourism that earns the locals their money.

Neither the owners of these centres, nor their guests seem to be interested in integrating themselves into the Greek village's community. The locals are the last to be informed when a new spiritual centre is established, which is sometimes even built without the necessary planning permission. There are hardly any Greek employees either and the "all-inclusive-standard" doesn't particularly support the local economy.

Martha, whose house was located not far from the Ouranos Club, had already laid the terrace table when Sophie arrived. Coffee and cake were ready and waiting. A medium-sized brown dog with a white spot on its chest was approaching her, wagging its tail and sniffing interestedly. Sophie knelt down and stroked him.

"I didn't ring the doorbell because the door was standing open already, I hope that was OK."

"Of course, our door is seldom closed, especially during nice weather, then the air can circulate better. Theo here lets everyone in. Whilst God was creating the watchdogs he was probably out playing," she laughed, "Oh, I'm so happy! Come and sit here, then you'll have a view of the sea."

"That island over there looks like a dragon lying in the water, sleeping. Look, left the snout and on the right the tail."

She pointed out to the sea.

"Yes, you're right. It's called Gravia, by the way. Oh, please have a piece, Kostas is taking our little one to her ballet lesson. That means we'll have a whole hour all to ourselves. The cake is from my mother-in-law, you just have to try it. By the way, blue suits you really well."

"Thanks, it's finally something other than the hospital white or dark green, right?" Sophie laughed, "You have really done well for yourself here. You're living on holiday. Thanks again for the invitation, Martha!"

"Well, it's not 'on holiday' if you actually live here, that's for sure. I also do some voluntary work in a hospital in town once a week. That's how I keep in practice and I'm also able to give something back to the people here. The local health system is really desolate, back in Germany, we tend to complain a lot, but compared to this... Even though it seems to be getting worse over there too, if you believe what the media says."

"That's very true, the shortage of nursing staff is getting progressively worse."

"Otherwise, I have enough to do during the season with the guests' apartments."

"You manage that all by yourself? Don't you have help with the cleaning?"

"Yes, I do. A young woman from our neighbourhood helps out. Oh, it's so good having you here, I wasn't really expecting you to come, to tell you the truth."

"Don't be silly! You know what it's like at the hospital. Everyone complains... And then, there's the weekend to cover, but you know all about that. Michael complains already that we don't have enough time for ourselves anymore. But what am I supposed to do? I love my job in Muenster. I think I already told you about Michael, didn't I?

"You certainly did. And it sounds very promising, even though a long-distance relationship wouldn't be my first choice..."

"It isn't mine either. Not permanently anyway, that's for sure. It's okay for the moment, though. I can find work in Kiel later, they're always in search of new doctors. But I'm not quite ready yet. You know, I've already been disappointed once."

"Couldn't Michael just move to Muenster?"

"No, I wouldn't want to drag him away from his beloved sailing and on top of that, his parents aren't the youngest anymore and he doesn't have any siblings. But let's talk about something else now... Mm, this cake is absolutely delicious."

"I'd love to pass on that compliment, but I'm sure you'll be able to do that by yourself later on."

"I probably won't be eating that much though, later," Sophie said, pointing towards her stomach.

"Oh, stop moaning about that! You with your model figure! Just have a look at me. Since my pregnancy I have must have gained about ten kilos, and I mean it."

"That actually suit you quite well, if you ask me!" Sophie laughed.

"That's what Kostas says, too ... But I'd still be happier without them ... So, what do you think of him?"

"I'm sure he's the right man for you ... Well, at least from what I have seen so far."

"I don't mean Kostas," Martha grinned, "I'm talking about Rolf."

"Rolf?" Sophie frowned.

"Yes, Rolf." Martha laughed.

"What are you laughing about? I think he's quite nice ... anyway, I hardly know him. Although he was behaving kind of strange earlier."

"Strange? Rolf?"

"Yes, he was standing on the terrace ... and somehow ... I don't know how to put this ... He was somehow spaced out, like he was in another dimension."

"What do you mean?"

"Well, it was like he was far, far away ... Even when I spoke to him, he needed a while to orientate himself ... You know, like someone who had just woken up after a general anaesthetic ... Oh, I really don't know how to explain it. It doesn't really matter anyway."

"Maybe he was contemplating a new motive for his pictures. He is a photographer after all and a good one at that. He has already had several exhibitions in Kerkyra. I think there's one running still and in Germany there are supposedly several art galleries showing his work."

"That's probably it then." Sophie went back to eating her cake again.

"Anyway, what's going on at the hospital? How are the colleagues? I haven't been in touch with anyone of late. I don't have any contacts there anymore. Is everyone still there?"

"Yes, Dr. Hansen is still there," Sophie grinned, "He's even got engaged."

"Really? Well, that's good to hear. It wouldn't have worked out between the two of us. We were just too different."

"I think he's quite nice."

" 'Quite nice' isn't enough to make a marriage work, Sophie. Furthermore, we only had three things in common: work, work and work." Martha giggled, "I have a few more points of interest with Kostas. He's such a wonderful man and I am happy to have him. He's got his heart in exactly the right place."

"As a cardiologist you're definitely the best judge of that." Sophie smiled, "But no, honestly. I'm so happy for you and I was able to see that right from the start."

"By the way, your farewell gift has got pride of place in the living room, I'll show it to you later."

"That's good to hear. To be honest, it was Dr. Hansen's idea."

"Really? I wasn't aware of that. Please tell him I'm grateful for it and that it was a shame he couldn't attend my farewell party ... Good grief, everything is so far away. Do you remember that unpleasant herpes I had?"

"I certainly do, and nothing ever seemed to help. None of the creams or pills... The things you'd tried."

"Then wait for it - since I've been kissing the *right* man, it's gone. Not a single, teeny, weeny blister. What do you say to that?"

"Hang on, you're asking me? Which one of us is the specialist in psychosomatics?"

"Hey, you two! How are you?"

Kostas gave Martha a kiss and the little Maria climbed onto her lap.

"You picked exactly the right moment", Sophie told him.

23

"Why?"

"We were just talking about you - only good things, of course."

"I hope my wife won't tell you the rest, either. Right, Agapi Mou?"

"And how old are you already, Maria?" Sophie asked her.

"I'm four years old." beamed the little girl, proudly holding up four fingers.

"And you probably speak Greek perfectly too, don't you?"

"Yes, we raise her bilingually," Martha answered. "I try to speak Greek only with Kostas, which sometimes proves to be difficult, seeing how good he is at German."

"Although your Greek is just about as good as my German now. Do you like your room, Sophie?" Kostas asked her.

"Oh yes, absolutely. Especially the great view and the tranquillity. By the way, are there any mosquitoes?"

"No, there shouldn't be very many in May, but I can give you a net anyway, I'll get it right away."

Martha stood up. Then she asked "Do you ride a motor scooter? If so, you really should rent one to get around better. They are really good fun. Kostas, could you call Pegasus and reserve one for Sophie?"

"Sure thing ... If you want to, Sophie."

"Absolutely. While I was a student I had a Vespa, so I'm not a learner."

"Fine, I'll ask Nikos to bring one here, I'll phone him right away. Though you must be careful, there are a lot of potholes in the area and the road is like an ice rink after a rainfall. Martha has had to treat the guests almost on a weekly basis. There are more than fifty lethal accidents involving tourists on Corfu every year. It is usually a combination of lack of experience, alcohol and high spirits. A lot of people also only wear light clothing and no helmet, too."

"I'll be careful. I promise."

CHAPTER 4

For those of you who are becoming en-lightened: Everything that you learn, you will begin to feel in your soul; and your companions, wherever they might be, will start to tremble at these sublime teach-ings. Something in you is beginning to yearn. They don't know what it is, but they start feeling marvellous about themselves. They don't know why, they just do. You share the emotions with them. This way, the souls of your soul mates are granted understanding, and they'll wake up. And very soon, for no reason, they will understand that they are the ones responsible for their own lives, and this truth will set them free. Free! (Ramtha)

Sunday

"**G**ood morning, sleepy head! You certainly had a lot of sleep to catch up on! How was your first night?"

"Uh.. it was quite good, thanks. But ..." Sophie said, glancing at her wristwatch, "... it's only nine o'clock." Martha was standing in the open terrace door.

"No, it's ten already. We're an hour ahead here, but no matter. Or do you have an operation on your agenda?"

"Oh no, I forgot to put my watch forward! Oh well, then it's ten already," Sophie laughed, "I slept like a log, wonderful, if you don't count that half an hour I spent with a mosquito that's now on its way to heaven. This peacefulness, only the chirping of the grasshoppers. The barking dogs didn't bother me at all, I'd go mad at home if the neighbour's dogs start barking at night."

"You're right, somehow it just seems to fit in here, I got used to it fairly quickly too. I don't even hear it anymore. Did you have any dreams? You know, the first dream in different surrounding often gets fulfilled."

Sophie laughed out loud.

"If that's right, my life would be in total chaos, that's for sure."

"Let's have breakfast then and you can tell me all about it. Maria's already in nursery school and Kostas has gone out fishing with a friend."

They had tomatoes, sheep cheese, fresh bread, home-made jam and a strong, Greek coffee.

"These tomatoes are absolutely delicious, Martha. You don't get them like this at back home in Germany, only watery ones."

"They're from Maria's garden. She grows just about everything. Potatoes, melons, onions, lettuce. She's even got hens, turkeys, sheep and goats. Nearly everything you get to eat here, is completely organic ... Well, except for the coffee and the bread."

"Wonderful, you have really landed on your feet, Martha, your in-laws are also so friendly, you can really tell how much they like you. It was a very pleasant evening with them yesterday."

"Well, I did present them with their very first granddaughter", Martha laughed. "Kostas sister has two boys, but joking apart ... they do really like me, they adopted me into their family right away. Even though Maria did help a little."

"Is naming your children after their grandparents' tradition here?"

"Yes, it's quite common."

"What did your mother think of it?"

"Oh, she was totally fine with it, more so than with the fact that I was moving to Greece, actually. Once they had visited us here for our wedding, she seemed happy with that, too. I did send you the pictures from our big day, didn't I? It was such a pity you couldn't come. We had two hundred guests! My parents are coming again soon, by the way, after you have left. They've been to Corfu ten times already since I moved here ... During his last visit, my father told me, *see, you can't get rid of us that easily!*

"But now tell me about your dream."

"I won't be able to recall everything though; it really was a mess.."

"No problem, aren't dreams always like that? Just start at the beginning!"

"Well, the thing I remember most clearly is probably that I'm standing at a harbour, watching old ships ... you know, those really old ones, made from timber and with colossal sails. Then, suddenly I start crying, I don't know why, but I was completely distraught. Then at the next moment I was shearing sheep and I was still crying. An old lady comforted me and said something, but I couldn't understand her. Then, she hugged me and gave me something ... a little animal, carved out of wood ... I think it was a dog ... that's when I woke up. There was more to the dream though, something to do with a cave, but I can't remember any more. Strange, don't you think?"

"Now, that's a case for Dr. Heuss, he could probably tell you what it's all about."

"Oh, he left us, by the way. He's now running a psychiatric department somewhere in Hamburg."

"Well, if you ask me, your dream has something to do with a kind of sad farewell," Martha concluded.

"Hmm, I am not too sure about that. Who sails on big old ships these days?"

"Maybe it's something from an earlier life."

"Earlier life? Do you now believe in stuff like that? You really have changed!" Sophie commented, smiling.

"Why? A lot of people believe in reincarnation, almost every religion in fact."

"That may be true, but ... Nobody has been able to prove that yet. I'm a scientist, I need evidence."

"Apparently, there is now some evidence, imagine that! Read the book 'Scientists confirm Reincarnation'. Just recently I attended the lecture of an American psychologist here in the Ouranos Club. He works with reincarnations, on a therapeutic basis."

"What is that supposed to be?"

"He explained that it can help coping with a trauma if you look into your past life to see whether the trauma originates from there. You know me from way back in the hospital, we have the same background, Sophie, but since I moved here, my view on certain things has taken a U-turn ... And I'm happy about that. But let's leave that behind us, you're here to enjoy your holidays, aren't you?"

"Yes, you're right, Martha, and I really do have the impression I can recharge my batteries here. There was an awful lot going on at work recently."

"Isn't it always like that?"

"You've got a point there. I think I'll have a very lazy day today. I saw a hammock out at the front of my apartment, would it be alright if I use it? I brought my Kindle and I'd like to read a bit, or just listen to an audio book."

"Of course, feel free, I've already stocked the fridge up for you. If you need anything, just come over and let me know. You won't have to go out for anything today."

CHAPTER 5

Anyone who hears a voice in their head, immediately thinks that they are a channel or a medium. He is not one. Why can't you accept the fact that it is your own knowledge. That is what you are hearing.
If you were to ask yourselves, the God of your being, he is knowledgeable; he has the answers. As soon as you ask another it is always a useless game, a puzzle, a speculation. (Ramtha)

Monday

When Rolf looked up from his book he immediately saw Sophie on the opposite side of the road waving, as she stood under the red flags of the *Ammos*. She was wearing white shorts and a bilious green shirt. A colourful beach bag was hanging from her shoulder. The sun was shining from a cloudless sky. It was early in the afternoon.

"Does she mean you, or me?" asked Leo Kaloudis, the proprietor of Ammos, grinning. He was sitting at the table behind Rolf and was preoccupied with his mobile phone.

"I hope she means me!" laughed Rolf. "I'm sure she doesn't know you yet, because she only arrived yesterday. I picked her up from the airport. She is staying at the Moustakas. She used to be a colleague of Martha's at the clinic."

Rolf waved back and Sophie crossed the road.

"May I join you, or would I be disturbing you? You're reading."

"Of course you may, how was the water?"

"To be quite honest, it was too cold for my liking, but the loungers are very comfortable ... and even with a waiter service"

Sophie sat down.

"Then you had better come in August, September or October, the sea is almost as warm as bathwater then."

"If only I had so much holiday ... but maybe I can convince my boyfriend to come along too ... next year and then in September."

Well, that's that out of the way, thought Rolf and smiled to himself.

"No camera today?" smiled Sophie.

"Aha, Martha has been gossiping!"

"Yes, she said you take terrific photographs."

"Perhaps ... they are alright, but there's quite a lot of room for improvement. I turned my hobby into my profession, but right now I am having a creative break, I read, swim, do a little yoga, go cycling, that sort of thing."

"I'd like to have it that easy too," Sophie sighed. "At the moment I can't afford to ... but for two weeks that's what I'm going to do. What are you drinking? It looks like blood! Martha never mentioned that you were a vampire."

Both had to laugh.

"Don't worry Sophie, I'm not a vampire. It is pomegranate juice. Very tasty, not too sweet and very refreshing. Would you like me to order you one? It's on me."

"May I try it first?"

"Yes, of course." Rolf passed her his glass.

"Interesting," Sophie commented. "Yes, I'll have the same ... it tastes a little bit bitter, thanks for the invitation."

"And how was your first night? Did you sleep well?"

"Oh yes ... well, not the whole night, a mosquito managed to get through the net. That was then the end of the peaceful night's sleep."

Rolf laughed, *"A wise man once said: If you think you are too small to make a difference, spend the night with a mosquito."*

"Well he was absolutely right!" she laughed too. "I didn't leave the grounds at all yesterday; I somehow slept the whole day. From the hammock to bed and back again, it is wonderful up there amongst the olive trees ... the tranquillity."

"Then you were in sore need of it! Martha has often spoken to me about your stressful work. Have you already eaten? They have some really tasty dishes here. If I had known you would show up, I would have waited with my salad."

"No, Thanks, I had fruit with me ... cherries. They're my favourite. I went to the grocer's this morning with Martha ... somewhere beyond Arillas."

"What?, You too? Cherries are my favourite fruit too! My grandparents had a cherry tree in their garden. That was the best for me ever. I don't recall how often I had stomach-ache due to eating too many of them.

My grandmother could warn me as often as she liked!" laughed Rolf. "I always buy my fruit at that shop too."

"And my grandmother had a saying: *Eaten cherries, drunk water, stomach-ache, dead.* I had to study medicine first before I realised that the saying wasn't true!" Now Sophie was laughing too.

"And I thought the same until just now!" grinned Rolf. "May I see what you are reading? Sorry about being nosy, but I love books. It's a good job there are E-readers, otherwise I would have had to have brought a second suitcase with me and that one would have been really heavy!"

Rolf held the book out to her.

" '*The Red Lion*' by *Mária Szepes*, a Hungarian author, have you heard of it?"

"No, I've haven't. What's it about?"

"Hmm, it's hard to say, I haven't quite finished it, but it is definitely very exciting. Let me see, in the sixteenth century a young alchemist called Hans Burger discovered the *Red Lion*. This was a powder that was supposed to give eternal life. However, he must kill in order to obtain the precious substance.

"What follows is an endless and very dramatic journey through the centuries, one during which he cannot escape from criminality. That is the price that has to be paid for being able to consciously remember all your past lives."

"By coincidence, we were discussing the concept of reincarnation at breakfast time, Martha is a firm believer of it."

"Do you believe in coincidences? I don't."

Sophie laughed. "What is going on here? First Martha, now you ... do you all belong to a sect?"

"A sect? No, of course not, you don't have to be in a sect to believe in it. Earlier in life I thought the same as you. I went to a technological university and wasn't taught such things."

"So, what did you study?"

"Architecture. I wanted to be a famous architect, like my father ... but at some point I realised that it wasn't my calling. We were more occupied with rules and the community regulations, there was no scope for creativity. I'm a lot better of working as a photographer. I am my own boss, if you like. I have always enjoyed photography. When I was seven years old my grandfather gave me a small Polaroid camera for Christmas. You wouldn't believe how I managed to get on everyone's nerves with it! No one was safe from me!" he laughed.

"Somehow I feel the same," said Sophie, thoughtfully. "In the clinic the work is getting more and more bureaucratic. Reports to the insurance companies and the like ... there is far too little time left to look after the patients. And that is the actual reason I chose that line of work, to be able to help people."

"Then you know what I am talking about."

"I certainly do ... and how did you manage to make the change? I mean, you live here, and you are a photographer."

"I was lucky ... or fate was good to me. I received an inheritance from my grandparents. That made it all a lot easier and I was able to follow my heart's desire. Would you like another juice?"

"No, thank you. I must get going, Martha's waiting. I promised to pick Maria up from nursery school with her and this evening they have invited me out for a meal ... somewhere in Afionas."

"Then you're probably going to *Panorama* or to the *Three Brothers*. As well as having an excellent meal, you have an amazing view of the sunset from there. I expect you'll be sitting outside, it's quite warm for the middle of May. Normally you'd still need a pullover in the evenings, but that won't be a problem seeing as though you brought one with you."

Rolf ordered a coffee from the waitress.

"What led to your change of heart? I mean, going from architecture to reincarnation, coincidence and fate, that's a big step."

"Don't you have to go? Or will an abridged version suffice?" he joked.

"I have enough time for that," Sophie answered, drinking up the last few drops of her juice.

"After I gave up architecture I went travelling ... aside of other countries, I also visited India and Nepal. I discovered a completely different world there. Have you already been there?"

"No, not yet, but it's on my list."

"For the people there, the idea of reincarnation is completely normal, as is believing in destiny, or, as they call it, *karma*. I guess if you told a Hindu something about the free will that we're all so proud about, he'd say: *That's your holy cow.*"

"Yes, but has reincarnation been proved yet? I mean, can we be sure about it?"

"Are you a Christian?"

"Yes, I think so ... But what does that have to do with it?"

"Because God isn't proven either. Do you actually think Maria was a virgin? I'm quite interested in hearing your opinion on that, you being a doctor."

"You have a point there, I must admit. No, I don't believe she was, but I think that was only told that way to emphasize how special Jesus was... And that he really existed, I guess."

"That's how I see it, too. In the Bible, there are even indications that, to the people of the past, the thought of rebirth wasn't entirely unfamiliar. In ancient Greece, this idea was widely spread. Only in the council in the year 553 A.D., if I recall it rightly, the theory of the transmigration of souls was banned. Which is obvious if you to sell people indulgences."

"To be honest, that does seem logical." Sophie smiled, "How do you know about all of this?"

"I read a lot. You know, I have time on my hands."

"I'd love to continue this conversation, but I must go now," she reached out for her swimming bag, "And again, thanks a lot for the invitation ... and this conversation. It was interesting."

"You're welcome! It was a pleasure ... Have fun this evening. Greet your hosts from me, will you?"

Rolf watched her as she left the Ammos, stowed the bag, put on her helmet, got on her motor scooter and drove away.

In the first couple of days they almost always wear a helmet, he thought.

"She's nice, isn't she?" Leo couldn't hide the fact he was grinning.

"She certainly is." Rolf answered and reached for his book again.

"Have you fallen in love?" Leo smirked.

Rolf looked up from his book.

"Fallen in love? Me? With whom?"

"Ha-ha, who do you think? That's the first woman I've seen you spending time with in ... wait a moment ... like, a year. And you seemed very close, if I may say so."

"Very funny, Leo. You've only had your Ammos open for two weeks and it has been closed since October. Probably because of being so well off, ha-ha."

"Yes, but that doesn't make any difference about my ability to judge character. A landlord is an expert at that. During the season, a lot of couples come here, some are in love, some aren't, and some don't even know it yet. Believe me, you develop a talent for it. And Sophie is nice ... and pretty."

"Aha, so you know her name already, too?"

"Listen, I was sitting directly behind you! She could open up a clinic here." Leo grinned again.

"Oh yes, and I'm sure Dr. Papadopoulos and his wife Tania, who is also a doctor, would be really enthusiastic about that."

"Then in St. Stephanos, they don't have a doctor there."

"Will you stop planning other people's futures for them?!" Rolf answered laughing. He liked Leo, their friendship went back a long time.

38

"I only want what's best for you!" Leo raised his hands in pretend indignation, "Anyway, you really should take a photo of her. Have you noticed that she almost looks Greek?"

He's got a point there, Rolf had to admit.

"Maybe I will ... Only if she wants to, though."

His mobile phone rang.

"Speak of the ... it's Angeliki, my gallery manager, I wonder what she wants. Incidentally, I was here once with her too."

He answered the call.

"Good morning Rolf, how are you? We haven't spoken for a while. Are you still on your creative break?"

"Hello Angeliki, thank you, I'm fine … and yes, my creative interlude, is going to last a little longer ... it's only been three weeks."

"Maybe not for much longer," she mused.

"Why not?"

"Are you sitting down?"

"Yes, I'm at Ammos, you know, where we were the last time we met. Come on, what are you going to tell me?"

"OK, you are going to have to come by, fairly soon if you can manage it. There's someone who wants to meet you."

"You are making this very exciting..."

"Well it is! Listen ... Yesterday there was a group of Japanese tourists in the gallery. A certain Mr. Amida Takahashi was particularly taken by your olive series. He could hardly contain himself for excitement. He was still standing in front of them with his wife after all the others had left."

"That's good to hear..."

"Hang on a minute, it gets even better. He bought them all and would like you to do an exhibition in Tokyo, in any case, he wants to meet you. He is the editor-in-chief of an important newspaper there. Rolf this is a major breakthrough!"

"Wow! Now that is a good piece of news ... I'll have to let that sink in for a bit first."

"Well don't take too long about it, Mr. Takahashi is leaving on Sunday ... he's waiting at his hotel for my answer. That is also where he has suggested meeting."

"Where is he staying then?"

"In the Corfu Palace."

"I should have known that!"

"Rolf, this is a chance of a lifetime you don't want to miss. Imagine, you could have an exhibition in Japan!"

"But only if I don't have to go there myself," he laughed.

"I can go there for you; I have always wanted to visit Japan. Please say that you will meet up with him!"

"Yes of course ... even if it is only for your sake!"

"You're an angel."

"I know," laughed Rolf. "I'll call you back later, but you can tell Mr. ... What was his name again?"

"Amida Takahashi."

"OK, I'll google the meaning of his name later, as far as I remember they find that important in Japan."

"You do that. I'll wait for you to call me back. Take care ... See you soon. I'm happy for you!"

"Good news?" asked Leo.

"Oh yes, I think so. Imagine, a Japanese tourist has bought some of my pictures. Do you have something to write with? I have to note a name down."

"Congratulations!"

"Thank you."

"What are you doing this evening? We are having the mushroom risotto that you like so much."

"Of course, that is very tempting, Leo, but I have to home. I am going to spend the evening sorting pictures and relaxing on the terrace, it's going to be a wonderful sunset."

Three hours later Rolf had finished his sorting and had taken a glass of wine, bread and sheep's cheese out onto his terrace, which looked out over the harbour in Arillas. When he had finished eating, he took his book and made himself comfortable in his hammock.

It was by *David duChemin* and was entitled '*The Soul of the Camera: The Photographer's Place in Picture-Making.*' He was a great admirer of the author who had been a photographer working internationally for a long time. Two more of his works stood alongside the literature of other well-known photographers in his bureau. *Maybe I will write a book one day too,* he thought to himself tiredly. Then he closed his eyes to contemplate a suitable title.

"Helena, I thought you weren't going to come ... look the bread has already gone dry."

It is supposed to sound like a reprimand, but it doesn't come across that way, because he is so in love with her. She knows that, because she loves him too.

The peaceful olive grove slopes down towards the sea, which, from so high up, looks like a pale blue strip of silk, stretched out between the island and the mainland. Grasshoppers are chirping in the branches of the pines and the olive trees, the bees humming fills the air and large colourful butterflies sated with sweet nectar flutter drunkenly in the hot air.

Far away from the village, in the shadows of the gnarled olive tree with its many faces, under which they secretly met, is where he has spread out the old ragged blanket. Kleitos, with whom he watches over the sheep, lies panting not far off in the shadow of a giant walnut tree, his watchful eyes never leaving the small herd. Next to a half-loaf of bread lay a small bottle of golden olive oil and a handful of dark red tomatoes. These have long since been discovered by a company of ants. With a flick of his hand he brushes the unwanted guests away. The sun is glaring mercilessly down from a cloudless sky.

He is wearing a pair of black shorts that are already full of holes, his naked torso is deeply tanned from the sun and glistening with a fine film of sweat, so that he appears to have been cast in bronze. She admires this image of him for a moment, then puts down the bundle of small branches and twigs she has been gathering on the way to one side and combs through his curly black hair with her fingers.

"Nikos, you know how attentive my father is. If he knew that we were meeting each other ... I swear by the Gods, he would kill you."

"But it would be worth dying for!" he laughs.

"Please, don't say things like that!"

She unpacks a piece of sheep's cheese out of its greasy wrapper and hands it to him with a smile that makes his heart swell with its sweetness.

"Here, take this ... I stole it from the larder ... and give me the bread, I like the dry crusts the best ... you know that! Come here Nikos, give me a kiss!"

They kiss, and time stands still.

"I have to go home Nikos," she whispers into his ear after they had made love." The old granny is surely looking for me already and if I'm not found by five o'clock then my father will come looking for me with the dogs!"

"I'll kill Lamia, if she betrays you, the old witch!"

"And what then? What will you do then Nikos? Do you want to be sent to prison ... for the rest of your life ... our lives? She only does what my father demands of her. She won't come up here on her old legs, it is too far and too steep. We are safe under our tree my love, it protects us, believe me."

CHAPTER 6

Even though many of you have come here in the desperate attempt to find your soul mate, did you know that the search involves enslavement and limitations? On the contrary the admission of a soul mate into one's sphere grants unlimited life. Do you understand? It works as follows: Once you have found out that such a being is hiding somewhere and you start to pull down the barriers that you have been building up for yourselves your whole life, then that soul will begin to speak to you on an emotional level, that is the manner in which they communicate. (Ramtha)

"It is so beautiful here," enthused Sophie, whilst they were sitting eating their meal on the large terrace of the *Three Brothers* in Afionas.

"That is what I promised," commented Martha, "There are any number of places like this here on the island. We wouldn't be able to show you them all, even if you were to stay here for half a year, isn't that right, my love?"

Kostas looked up from his plate. He had taken the car and joined them later, because he had been helping a friend who was building a house and he wasn't sure whether he would otherwise make it before sunset. For that reason, the two women had taken Sophie's motor scooter, which they had parked right next to the entrance of the tavern.

"That's right," he replied, "But I think you probably know Corfu better than I do now. You know Sophie, she tours the island with everyone who comes to visit us. Her parents alone have been to visit at least ten times."

"Oh, look! The sun is setting!" called Sophie excitedly, "What a beautiful view! What are those islands over there?"

"You know the sleeping dragon already, the closest, that is Gravia. The larger one behind it is *Mathraki*, the flat one to the right is *Erikousa* and a little further out is *Othoni*. You really must visit the islands," claimed Martha, "There's hardly any tourism, just picturesque beaches and delightful little villages. Mathraki has a beautiful beach, almost like in the Caribbean and at the harbour there is a pub with delicious food. Higher up there is a quaint little village with a pretty little church. It all looks just how it must have done a hundred years ago."

"The beach at Erikousa is also very beautiful," added Kostas. "We go fishing in the waters around these islands."

"Could you possibly take me with you one day?" asked Sophie, hopefully.

"Unfortunately, we are not allowed to take tourists out, but there is a post-boat that sails out there twice a week from St. Stefanos. I can show you the harbour tomorrow if you like."

"What?" interrupted Martha, "Then ask Rolf!"

"Rolf?"

"Yes, he owns a boat, just ask him."

"Err ... I don't know ..."

"What don't you know?"

"But he will think I'm too intrusive, he has already offered to guide me around this island a bit ... no he didn't ... it was you who suggested he did that!" smiled Sophie, pointing to her friend with her fork.

"Yes, it was, so what? He didn't seem to put off by the idea and he has plenty of time. As far as I can remember, he is not currently doing any photography."

"That's right he is having a creative break... he told me about it today."

"I see," grinned Martha. "You met up with each other already?"

"What are you grinning about? We didn't have a date. When I left the beach, he was sitting in Ammos and invited me for a drink. Anything wrong with that?"

"Nowt!" said Martha and winked at her husband. Sophie, however, noticed the look.

"Martha, will you stop it? You know that I have a boyfriend at home!"

"As far as I recall, he is not at home, but in Kiel. But I didn't say you should go and get engaged to Rolf or anything! I'm sorry."

"It's alright," Sophie stroked Martha's arm, "I know that you only have the best intentions for me. By the way, the calamari is delicious."

"This restaurant is a real family business," mentioned Kostas, who wasn't keen on the way the conversation was developing. "The father, Vassilis Bardis is the chef and the mother, Aliki, along with their daughters, Georgia and Urania, do the waiting on. You'll see in a minute that they are twins. We love coming here. By the way, they rent out apartments too ... just up there."

"Oh? Do you want to get rid of me already?" joked Sophie.

"No! I didn't mean it like that!"

"Oh, what a relief! ... I know you didn't mean it like that!"

Sophie's mobile rang.

"A second please, it's Michael ... I'll just go over there a moment, you carry on eating, OK?"

Sophie stood up and moved a couple of metres to one side where no other guests were sitting.

"Hello Michael, how are you?"

"I'm fine, I just wanted to hear how you are. You arrived safely then?"

"Yes, of course ... I sent you a WhatsApp yesterday ... it is wonderful here; you should see it. We are just having dinner and have experienced the most beautiful sunset."

"So, who is 'we'?"

"Martha, Kostas and me. Why? Is anything the matter? You sound sort of, strange."

"Because you usually call in the evening before you go to bed, but yesterday you didn't."

"Oh, love, we were invited to dinner at Martha's in-laws and it was very late, so I didn't want to wake you, you were most probably already asleep."

"No, I wasn't."

"I'm sorry then love, from now on I'll call then ... I promise ... or you call me ... but remember, we are an hour ahead here. Listen, I must get back to the others, they're waiting and my dinner's getting cold. Take care and big hug!"

Sophie rang off and went back to the table.

"What's the matter?" asked Martha, "You look like you have found a penny and lost a pound."

"Michael was a bit weird just now, I've never experienced him like that before."

"What do you mean by weird?"

"I don't know ... just, funny."

"Is he jealous?"

"Well, yes, sometimes. If he is in Kiel and I am in Muenster we call each other at least once a day and always in the evening ... except when I am on night duty. But then he knows that usually. To be quite honest with you, sometimes I get the impression he's checking up on me. But if that remains the only thing that annoys me then that's alright, everything else is fine. Admittedly, I have never experienced him like this before."

"Maybe he notices something."

"What should he have noticed?"

"Oh, nothing, just eat your Pastitzada, otherwise it will get cold, I hope you like them."

"It is delicious," answered Sophie, chewing. "Would you mind if I tried your lamb?"

"Of course, here, take some.

"Oh, that is so tender and so tasty, I'll order that dish next time."

"If you like grilled lamb," said Kostas, "You must definitely go to *Mon Amour* in Kavadades for dinner one time. That is one of the oldest taverns in the area ... I think it is already in its fourth generation. For a few years now the *Athina*, on the way out of Arillas, is also commendable. Though it doesn't have a top location, the tavern boasts very good food and has friendly service."

"Mon Amour, what a lovely name."

"The female members of the family, Katina and Iliana cook and grill the food with a good portion of love," said Martha. "That tavern should definitely on the list of compulsory visits for all tourists. Fortunately, they are open through the winter. So, if I can't be bothered to cook, we usually go there."

Kostas laughed: "There aren't that many other possibilities here!"

"Too true! The pizzeria in Arillas is only open at the weekend and then there is *Kostas at the Beach* ... and that is about it ... Oh, yes, there is quite a good pizzeria in *Roda*, that's not too far from here."

After the meal Sophie said: "Please don't be angry with me, but I would like to be alone for a while. I'm going to go the bench that you recommended to me Martha. I'll find my own way back. After two glasses of wine I should manage it."

"Yes, you do that, I'll drive back home with Kostas and if you were to get lost, just give us a call, we'll come and find you."

CHAPTER 7

If you have begun the process of breaking down your boundaries, you can begin to live. Because life is an outstanding gift. So as soon as you start to take down the boundaries that you have built up for yourselves, then you are gradually recalling your power and pulling yourselves closer to your personal companions. Do you understand? (Ramtha)

Sophie only had to go a short way through the old village before she saw the three benches on the rise behind the restaurant *Anemos*. The terrace of the restaurant was full of guests and on passing by, Sophie thought it would be a nice place to eat too, she liked the look of it.

Then, it was completely tranquil. Martha had told her that usually at sunset there were usually any number of people here. Now, the waning half-moon hung in the sky and illuminated the islands that Sophie had already seen from the terrace of the restaurant the *Three Brothers*.

'The moon's silver streetlight', thought Sophie after she had sat herself down. She had seen the book on the children's ward of the hospital. Sometimes, when time permitted, the night duty nurse would read one of the stories to the little patients. Afterwards they usually all slept quite well.

All that could be heard now was the chirping of the grasshoppers, somewhere in the village dogs were barking. Now she was thankful that she had taken the thin pullover with her.

The sleeping dragon, she just managed to think as she was suddenly overcome by a wave of tiredness, just as though the wind had blown it over to her.

Maybe it was too much wine, she could barely think, then her eyes closed.

"Helena, come into the house at once, where have you been? Do you know how late it is?"

Her father is standing on the threshold and his expression is grim. The twilight has begun, and it is beginning to get cold. She pulls her shawl tight about her shoulders. She fears her father's fury and tries to appear as self-confident as possible.

"Papa, let me into the house please, I'd like to help mother, so that the evening meal is ready on time. I was at Eleni's house and helped her with the spinning. What is the matter Papa? Why are you so annoyed?"

"What's the matter? You ask what's the matter? Don't put on the innocent! Lamia was at Eleni's too, but you weren't there. Then Lamia searched the whole village for you."

"Then we must have just missed each other. I took the perimeter path to check on the goats, there are supposed to be wolves around."

"Aha, and so how are you going to explain why neither Georgos nor Alexis had seen you. The two of them have been with the herd all day because of the wolves."

Helena contracts her stomach sharply and tears shoot into her eyes. Usually she can soften up her father with this trick, but this time it is to no avail.

"You don't honestly think that I am ignorant of this impoverished shepherd, who doesn't even own a decent pair of trousers! You were seen with him a couple of days ago. You know that I have many eyes in the village. You can't hide anything from me!"

"But Papa," she tries to appease her father.

"Not, 'Papa', that doesn't work anymore. I can't chaperone you all day, I work hard to enable you to have the life that you have. You will marry a suitable man, one that I have chosen for you ... Yes, you did hear properly ... chosen for you! You will be meeting him quite soon. He comes from a very revered, wealthy family and you can think yourself very lucky, if he marries you. In future, you will only leave the house in the accompaniment of your mother or Lamia."

She can't hold back her tears any longer. She would much rather have told her father that she would prefer a simple life and be happy. But instead she turns around and flees.

I must tell Nikos, she thinks.

"You come straight back here!" her father calls after her, "I'm going to kill that man!"

But she must go to Nikos to tell him that they won't be able to see each other for a few days. Afterwards they will surely find a way to escape her chaperones. She has no lack of imagination.

Sophie's eyes snapped open in astonishment. The sea was just as peaceful as it had been before. She was breathing heavily, and she stood up. She looked around, but everything seemed completely normal. *What on earth just happened? An unbelievable day-dream ... with images that were crystal clear, so different to usual dreams.*

She checked her watch and realised that she had spent more than an hour in that strange trance.

Did they put something in my wine? I have never experienced anything like that before. I was dreaming without being asleep!

She stretched and inhaled deeply a couple of times.

If I tell Martha what happened, she will think I have gone mad!

She turned around a looked for her motor scooter.

Oh, you idiot, I left it at the Three Brothers. I really must wake up now.

As she drove past *Anemos* little while later, there were still some tourists sitting together and talking to each other quite animatedly.

What a difference to just now, thought Sophie, *I was in a completely different world.*

She paused for a moment, wondering whether to have something else to drink.

"Come on in!" called Spiro, the landlord, "We are open for another half hour."

There's another Greek who speaks perfect German, she thought.

"Yes, thanks, I think I will, I really could do with a drink."

"I'll bring you an Ouzo, that's a remedy for everything."

"Whatever that is, I'll take one." smiled Sophie.

Tastes good, she thought a little later. *Anisette, I hope I'm still under the limit. 'Though I'm pretty sure there are no police about.*

An hour later she parked the scooter in front of the house and entered the apartment. Next door, everything was shrouded in darkness.

A piece of paper lay on her pillow.

Rolf asked whether you would like to drive into town with him tomorrow. He has a business appointment. If you would like to accompany him he would go to the 'White House' for breakfast. Go with him, you will enjoy it.

His number is: 0030 555789. He said you can send him an SMS and then he'd pick you up at nine. Sleep well and sweet dreams. I can't wait!

Love from your friend, Martha.

P. S. Michael called again. Your mobile was switched off. I told him everything was fine. That was OK, wasn't it?

Underneath, Martha had drawn a little heart.

Sophie reached for her mobile, which in the meantime she had put on to charge and wrote a WhatsApp to Michael.

"SORRY LOVE, BUT MY MOBILE WAS EMPTY. I HOPE YOU ARE ALRIGHT. MARTHA AND KOSTAS ARE SPOILING ME ROTTEN. SHALL GET IN TOUCH TOMORROW EVENING. X."

She wrote the next message to Rolf.

"THANK YOU VERY MUCH FOR YOUR INVITATION, I WOULD LOVE TO COME WITH YOU. BEST WISHES, SOPHIE."

Then she undressed and lay down under the mosquito net. The terrace door was wide open, from outside the chirping of the grasshoppers and somewhere the strange, hypnotic call of a bird was to be heard. Shortly afterwards, she fell asleep to their accompaniment.

CHAPTER 8

You and your soul mates are bound to each other for eternity. You are one God on an amazing journey. One God, who can express itself as both man and woman. You both always represent such a oneness, such a completeness, that it is neither masculine nor feminine, but both. And for 10 million years you have experienced this plane together. (Ramtha)

Tuesday

"Wakey, wakey! It's half past eight!" Martha was standing in the doorway, holding a cup of coffee, beaming.

Drunk from sleep, Sophie murmured: "Good morning, my word, you are always in a good mood! Thanks for the coffee, that's just what I need!"

"What on earth did you get up to? It must have been very late, because I didn't hear you come home."

"I'm not very sure, I think it must've been about one. I went back to Anemos to have another drink. It was such a lovely evening ... and anyway, I'm on holiday!" she grinned, "Which bird is it that has such a mono-tone call?"

"That is the little owl, who calls for its mate."

"It is not particularly creative." grinned Sophie.

"But insistent."

"Indeed, it is!"

"Listen, have you seen a black cat with four white paws anywhere about? I haven't seen our tomcat since Saturday. Kostas thinks that he is being bullied by a rival, who comes at night to steal his food. Admittedly he seems to have been eating a lot recently and our laundry room smells of cat urine, although *Mister Z* never pees inside the house."

"No, I haven't met Mister Z, lots of other cats, yes, but I will keep my eyes peeled."

She didn't want to tell her friend about her experience on the bench just yet.

"You can tell that you are on holiday already after only two days."

"Really?"

"Yes, look in the mirror. When I saw your pallor on arriving, I thought that this woman was working too hard. Now I know it for sure."

"Was it so obvious to see? My word. One never notices things like that oneself."

"You are doing the right thing ... and ... are you going with him to town?"

"Yes, I'm going to. Thanks for waking me up and for the note."

"My intuition told me, that you would go. Michael seemed to be a little worried, by the way. Did you speak to him again yesterday?"

"No, the battery needed charging. I really enjoyed the peace and quiet up there. Although I would have loved to have taken a photograph, the moonlight reflecting on the sea was so beautiful. But I'm sure that I will go up there again. It is not far with the scooter, although on the way back I was freezing, despite the jumper I had on. I think I will leave my mobile at home for the next couple of days, it's just annoying."

"That is a good idea." In the meantime, Martha had sat herself down next to Sophie on the bed, pushed the mosquito net back and had given her the cup of coffee.

"With milk and sugar was right, wasn't it? I didn't pay much attention yesterday, but in the clinic that's how you took it."

"Yes, that's right. I just can't force myself to drink it black, although that is supposed to help your looks."

"As if you need any help on that score! I think it is a good idea that you are going along too, Rolf really is a good tour guide."

"And, so what are you grinning about?"

"I wasn't grinning."

"Yes, you were."

"I was just thinking my thoughts." she said.

"Yes, and you can keep them to yourself!" Sophie nudged her friend in the side.

"Do you have a bad conscience?"

"Me? Why? Towards whom?"

"Hey, stop putting it on. Michael of course."

"Why should I? Rolf is your friend, I trust him."

"And you can too."

"Well then,, ... Oh, I think I just heard a car. Please tell him that I need another ten minutes, I'll be quick." Sophie hastily drank the last of her coffee and jumped out of bed.

There was probably no one on the island who didn't know the name *Durrell*. The family's house was located near the most north-eastern tip of the island at a place called *Kalami*.

It is still known as *The White House* today, is situated at the end of the local bay and is not only inviting in a culinary sense. There is a lounge with comfortable deckchairs underneath olive trees, where one can forget about time by watching water-skiers or the yachts casting anchor in the bay.

A day passes by quickly here.

During their three year stay here, the Durrell's had befriended the locals. They loved the island and its population and were loved back by them. They wrote books about Corfu, which they considered to be their paradise. The probably best-known book was titled *Prospero's Cell*.

On their trip to Kerkyra, Rolf and Sophie made a short stop in Kalami to have breakfast. During the drive Rolf had told her it was one of his favourite places on the island and that he really wanted to show it to her.

"Then I'd love to see it, Martha recommended visiting Kalami too, by the way. Thanks so much for taking me with you."

During their journey Sophie was very surprised with herself for feeling so familiar with Rolf. The day before in Ammos had been the same. She was usually more reserved when she met people for the first time. But Rolf made it easy for her, with his relaxed and genuine character.

"My pleasure, you wanted to go into town anyway. It is far too far with the motor scooter, you would be on the road for at least two hours ... in one direction. I have a business appointment regarding my photographs there today, so fits in quite well. You will have plenty of time to have a look around. You will like Kerkyra, but first we are going to the White House. It is very famous. The British author, Lawrence Durrell wrote one of his books there at the beginning of the last century. If you want to learn something about this island, I'd really recommend you read it. Perhaps they'll have it on sale there.

The apartment he had lived in has been maintained almost exactly how it was during the time he lived there, and it is even possible to rent it. I've been playing with the idea of staying there for a while for some time now. Maybe some of his inspiration would rub off on me." he laughed.

They found a shady space under a majestic olive tree. The comfortable loungers and swinging chairs were most inviting. A small table stood between them, set out with a simple breakfast of croissants and coffee. Several yachts and a catamaran were anchored in the bay, small motorboats were taking tourists to isolated beaches or the ones in the vicinity of the town Kassiopi.

"It is beautiful here!" said Sophie, "Thank you so much for showing it to me. I would never have found this on my own."

A short while later Rolf came back with a small, thin book.

"Here, look what I have got, Durrell's book, *Prospero's Cell*. It's a present for you."

"Oh, thank you very much! I'll be sure to read it, I'll start it tomorrow. I bet it's a perfect book for the beach."

"When I read the book for the first time several years ago ... I have often taken it to hand ... I thought of how often I had always hoped that an author would pen a description of this island. The language he uses, his experiences here and the intensity of the love he obviously felt towards the people here, impressed me deeply. He has literally photographed the island through his words. Would you mind if I read you the beginning of the book?"

"Be my guest. Now I'm really excited!"

"I quote from the beginning of the book, *Prospero's Cell*:

It is April and we have taken and old fisherman's house in the extreme north of the island - Kalami. Ten sea-miles from the town, and some thirty kilometres by road, it offers all the charms of seclusion. A white house set like a dice on a rock already venerable with the scars of wind and water. The hill runs clear up into the sky behind it, so that the cypresses and olives overhang this room in which I sit and write. We are upon a promontory with its beautiful clean surface of metaphoric stone covered in olive and ilex: in the shape of a mons pubis. This is become our unregretted home. A world. Corcyra. (Corfu)."

"That is truly magical ... such wonderful prose," said Sophie, "Thank you for the book, I'm sure I shall read it. Just now, I imagined how it must have looked back in the twenties, before the tourists came. Maybe it is easier to empathize with him if you were to live in his apartment with the little terrace overlooking the sea. Would you please read a little more?"

"Of course."

"It is a sophism to imagine that there is any strict dividing line between the waking world and the world of dreams. N. and I, for example, are confused by the sense of the several contemporaneous lives being lived inside us; the sensation of being mere points of reference for space and time. We have chosen Corcyra perhaps because it is an anteroom to Aegean Greece with its smoke-grey volcanic turtle-backs lying low against the ceiling of heaven. Corcyra is all Venetian blue and gold - and utterly spoilt by the sun. Its richness cloys and enervates."

Rolf closed the book and gave it to her.

"Many, many thanks! I'll start it first thing tomorrow at the beach."

She perused the book cover for a moment and then put the book in her beach bag.

"If we had had enough time we could have gone for a swim. The water here is especially clear. But we should almost get going, I have to be at the hotel for one o'clock."

Rolf began to pack his things into his small backpack.

"Is the art gallery there?"

63

"No, it's further away on the north side of town. A Japanese customer is waiting for me at the hotel. The owner of my gallery, Angeliki, made the appointment, she was ecstatic about it. Apparently he's bought several of my photographs and would like me to have an exhibition in Tokyo."

"Congratulations! That's wonderful!"

"Well, I'm not sure, but I'm going to hear what he has to say, if only for the sake of my friend, Angeliki. His name sounds very promising. I googled him yesterday evening. It's a good job that I still have a few visiting cards left, without them I probably shouldn't even bother turning up. But then again, maybe that is just a cliché."

"What is his name then?"

"Amida Takahashi. Amida is the Name of a Buddha and Takahashi means *High Bridge*."

"That sounds very good, "said Sophie, "Your bridge to Japan."

"That I will not be crossing. If he wants to exhibit my pictures though, he is very welcome to."

"What exactly do you photograph?"

"Mr. Takahashi bought my series entitled 'Olive trees,' consisting of twenty, large format pictures. The centrepiece of the series is one of the oldest olive trees in the world. On the initiative of a private union in *Strongili* it became one of the first certified natural monuments. It has the nickname "Evdokia" and has been heralded as one of the ten oldest olive trees worldwide. You can go and have a look at it. Apparently the oldest tree is on Crete, it is supposed to be three thousand years old. I didn't just photograph the trees though, I captured the people harvesting the olives, the oil presses ... everything that goes with it.

"I gave my last work the title 'Corfu's faces.' I photographed predominantly old people. Every face tells an interesting story ... completely free of Botox and all that rubbish that is so popular with us now!" he laughed.

"Oh, I would love to see all those pictures!"

"I have them all saved on my tablet, if you like I can show them to you later."

"That with the business cards is really important for the Japanese," smiled Sophie, "Some of my fellow students were Japanese, so I know a couple of their habits ... and since then I like Sushi too."

"What, you too? Then we should go and have some."

"What? There's a sushi restaurant here on Corfu?"

"There are two! However, I always go to the same one. They always get their fish fresh from the market, every day. Do you fancy it?"

"Whether I'd like to? What a question!"

"OK, then we'll go and eat sushi."

"I'd like to tell you something, do you think we still have enough time?"

Rolf paused a moment. "We'll simply make time."

"Something out of the text from Durrell's book moved me just now, when he wrote about the simultaneity of multiple existences in us ... Oh, I don't know how to put it, but yesterday evening, as I was sitting alone on a bench overlooking Afionas, I had a very strange experience. One that I have never had before."

Rolf had sat himself back down again facing Sophie, intrigued.

"I'm curious, what happened?"

"Nothing around me, but inside me."

Sophie recounted the story of what she had experienced the other evening.

"That was strange, don't you think? Hey, are you crying?

She had noticed tears in his eyes.

"I don't know ... I am certainly very moved by your story and I think I should confide something in you too.

"Now I'm the curious one ... but what do you think about my story?"

"Let me tell you about mine first, please. Can you remember the day you arrived? I was up on the terrace whilst you were unpacking your things. You then came out and asked me whether I was alright ..."

"Yes, I can remember, I even mentioned it to Martha."

"Whilst I was out there, looking through the olive trees towards the sea, I also had the daydream that I'm going to tell you about now. I can still remember all the exact details."

After Rolf's account, they both sat in silence for a while.

"Why didn't you tell me about it?" asked Sophie with a thick voice and tears in her eyes.

He reached for her hand, which she permitted without a word.

"Well for one thing, we had only been acquainted for about two hours and for another, I had no reason to connect any of it to you."

CHAPTER 9

If you do not love each other enough to become simple beings, you will die. It is as simple as that. You can make up all the excuses you like, you can blame everyone else for your fate, bit it will not change anything! And who created that? You! You make the difference. Saying "I cannot change myself" is an illusion. It is backing out: You do not want to change yourselves! (Ramtha)

After the unforgettable breakfast in the White House they drove along the picturesque coastal road to town. Sophie was permanently fascinated by the bays and olive groves. For the rest of the journey they didn't broach the subject of the daydreams that they had both experienced independently of each other, and in different locations.

"I think I know why you chose this island to be the epicentre of your life. Do you often have to go to Germany?"

"Should I?" laughed Rolf.

Sophie laughed too.

"I didn't mean it like that, I mean because of your pictures. You mentioned that you also exhibit them in Germany."

"Not often. I fly back maybe five or six times a year ... but not just because of the pictures, I also visit my family and friends. Not long ago I was at the wedding of a friend in Wiesbaden ... but maybe I'll have another reason to in future," Rolf glanced over to Sophie to check her reaction and swore to himself for saying it. But it had just slipped out, spontaneously.

"I don't think that would be a good idea. I have my own life in Germany and as you know, I'm in a relationship. Is there no woman in your life?"

"Not anymore, we went our separate ways the year before last. Susan couldn't get settled into life here and she missed Munich. At the beginning she was all for it, but then it became too boring ... especially after she had experienced a winter here. Furthermore, I had an important contract at the time, and I'd had a lot of work to do. So, one thing led to another ... Oh well, that's the way things go. The love wasn't strong enough. We are still friends though, incidentally she is getting married soon."

"Perhaps we should also leave that, which we've experienced, here too? I find it fits into the surroundings very well, don't you?"

"I think you are probably right ... No, you are definitely right."

"I thank you for that. How old are you by the way? Sorry for being nosy."

"That's OK, Sophie, I am pretty much exactly seven years older than you."

Sophie laughed, "I see, forty-two ... and so what else has Martha gossiped about?"

"Quite a lot," grinned Rolf. "No, only joking, not much else, other than that you were colleagues and that she likes you a lot ... Oh and that she was amazed that you managed to drag yourself away from your work."

"Well, the feeling is mutual, and she's right about the rest too. Not long ago I became a senior consultant and have even more responsibility now."

"Do you do social media?"

"No, I haven't enough time, anyway, I have no idea what I could post there. Do you do it?"

"Only Instagram, because of my pictures. The gallery managers insisted."

Sophie pressed his hand and he held it tight. So, they drove for the rest of the way into town, in silence, each of them occupied with their own thoughts.

"So here we are," said Rolf, as they pulled up outside the *Corfu Palace* Hotel. "This is where my appointment is. I doubt I'll need longer than an hour."

"Then I'll come along and pick you up," said Sophie. "I'll go for a walk along the promenade and take a look at the beautiful ships."

"Alright then, see you in an hour, then I'll show you some of the town and you simply must see the market."

The *Corfu Palace* is perfectly situated, just ten minutes' walk from the town centre. The five-star residence with a view over the *Garitsa Bay*, which is busy with yachts during the holiday season, boasts a Health Spa, an outdoor swimming pool and a gourmet restaurant. All the elegantly furnished rooms, which are reminiscent of the colonial era, enjoy the view of the Ionic sea.

At the reception, Rolf enquired after Mr. Takahashi.

"Mr. Takahashi awaits you in the lounge, Sir."

He ran up the broad steps to the lounge, where a single guest was sitting, preoccupied with a mobile telephone.

That must be him, thought Rolf, and approached the lone figure.

"Mr. Takahashi?"

"Oh, Mr. Rolf?" Herr Takahashi raised himself up out of his comfortable armchair. Rolf estimated him to be in his mid-fifties, but he also knew that with Asians it was very easy to be mistaken.

"Yes, Rolf Wendtland. I am pleased to meet you, Sir." Rolf had his visiting card ready and presented it respectfully with both hands.

Mr. Takahashi reciprocated the gesture to Rolf in the same manner, smiling.

"As you can see, I have a web-site, where you may see further pictures from my collections."

"I am certain I shall do that, but please, Mr. Wendtland, do take a seat. May I order you some refreshment?" said Mr. Takahashi in very good German and accentuated by a slight bow, after they had both examined the visiting cards for a moment. "A beer perhaps? This Corfu beer tastes wonderful." He indicated to the dark red bottle standing next to a half-filled glass on the table in front of him.

"Yes, it does indeed, Sir. Incidentally, this beer is brewed in the town in which I live, in Arillas."

"Oh, really?"

"Yes, I'll take a beer. If you were to return to this beautiful island, you must do so in October, that is when Arillas puts on its yearly beer festival - like a mini October festival."

"Oh, I'm sure this won't be the last time we come here, my wife enjoyed her stay too. By the way, she is still in the town and sends her apologies. I have already been to the Munich beer festival twice, The Japanese love that sort of thing!"

"I'm sure I'll make your wife's acquaintance, the next time you visit at the latest. First, I would like to express my thanks to you for purchasing my pictures ... and I must compliment you on your excellent German."

Herr Takahashi smiled; "I am sure you would speak Japanese just as well, if you were to live in Tokyo for ten years. I read Media Studies in Cologne. After a work placement at a large newspaper in Berlin, I returned to my home country to join my father's publishing house."

"I wanted to join my father's architecture business, but then I realised that it wasn't the right path for me."

"Well it is quite obvious that you have found the right direction now. You have the knack of it, if you permit me to say so. The Japanese understand much about photography." Mr. Takahashi laughed out loud.

In the meantime, the waiter had brought the beer over and had served him a glass.

"Let us drink to your success in Japan!"

Well, he is a little forward, thought Rolf. *That is not typical Japanese behaviour at all. It must be the German part of him coming out.*

"Please accept my most sincere apologies, if I am rushing you, Mr. Wendtland, but our return flight leaves on Sunday evening ... unfortunately."

"Oh, that is fine, I like people who don't beat about the bush."

Herr Takahashi laughed.

"So, what do you think about having an exhibition in Tokyo? You don't have to worry about doing any advertising, we shall do that. You will be subject of a large article.

Now he sounds like an American, mused Rolf.

"Of course, I would be greatly honoured indeed, Mr. Takahashi. However, I'd like to discuss the matter with my gallery manager, she deals with all my art business here and I would hate to go behind her back. I am sure you can appreciate that. would it be alright if she managed the deal, if it were to come to business?"

"But of course, Mr. Wendtland, discuss the matter with Mrs. Demetrio. You have my telephone number and I look forward to hearing your answer,"

Rolf stood up.

"Then that is settled then. If you would please excuse me I am afraid I have another important appointment ... please give my regards to your wife from me."

"I shall, she will be upset that she missed meeting you ... but then, maybe in Tokyo. Many thanks for the time you have taken."

The two men shook hands.

"I hope you enjoy the rest of your stay on the island ... and once again, many thanks, I feel very honoured."

"I should be thanking you, Mr. Wendtland. For letting me make your acquaintance."

Rolf wrote a WhatsApp in the hotel foyer.

"HELLO ANGELIKI, HAVE JUST MET MR. TAKAHASHI. DO YOU FANCY TRAVELLING TO TOKYO? I THINK THE EXHIBITION MAY COME OFF. REGARDS, ROLF."

The answer arrived the moment Rolf was leaving the hotel.

"HELLO ROLF, THAT IS ABSOLUTELY FANTASTIC! ARE YOU SURE YOU DON'T WANT TO GO TO TOKYO? I'D LOVE TO GO. I AM JUST PACKING YOUR PICTURES UP FOR MR. TAKAHASHI. HE WANTS TO TAKE THEM WITH HIM PERSONALLY. WITH THE POST IT TAKES TOO LONG:-) REGARDS, ANGELIKI."

In the meantime, Sophie had also been texting. She had sat for a while on a bench on the promenade, observed the yachts and had pondered over her experience in the White House. Then she extracted her phone, which she had actually intended to leave behind, out of her bag.

"HELLO MARTHA, I'D LIKE TO SPEAK WITH YOU TODAY IF YOU HAVE TIME. I HAVE TO TELL YOU SOMETHING."

IT DIDN'T TAKE LONG FOR MARTHA'S ANSWER TO ARRIVE.

"WHAT HAS HAPPENED? ARE YOU ALRIGHT? OF COURSE I'VE GOT TIME FOR YOU, JUST COME OVER WHEN YOU GET BACK. KOSTAS HAS GONE TO ACHARAVI WITH MARIA TO VISIT AN AUNT. HOW WAS IS IN THE WHITE HOUSE? IT'S GREAT THERE, ISN'T IT? BYE"

"IT WAS LOVELY AT THE WHITE HOUSE, IT REALLY IS A LOVELY PLACE, YOU WERE SO RIGHT! IN THE TOWN NOW. ROLF HAS GOT HIS MEETING AT THE HOTEL, LATER HE WANTS TO SHOW ME THE TOWN AND THE MARKET. I'LL TELL YOU WHAT HAPPENED LATER. SO LONG, S. ROLF WILL BE HERE SOON, I'LL CALL LATER."

"HEY, DON'T KEEP ME GUESSING!"

"THIS EVENING, MARTHA."

"OH, OK, ARE YOU GOING FOR SUSHI? I BET YOU ARE! YOU BOTH LOVE SUSHI AND THE YAMI IS REALLY GOOD."

"YOU CLAIRVOYANT, YOU:-)"

"WELL, THAT WAS REALLY HARD :-), HAVE FUN YOU TWO. SEE YOU LATER. I MUST GO NOW TOO. TAKE CARE, M"

"Well, how was your appointment?"

Rolf sat himself down next to her.

"Pretty successful I think. Mr. Takahashi is not typically Japanese," he grinned.

"What do you mean by that?"

"He didn't beat about the bush and came fairly straight to the point."

"That is certainly very unusual for the Japanese. That's what was so frustrating with my fellow Japanese students, how long it used to take them to get the message across." laughed Sophie.

"Maybe he feels pushed for time. He is departing on Sunday, on the other hand, he has lived in Germany for ten years."

"Does that mean you will have an exhibition in Japan? I'm so pleased for you."

"It looks that way doesn't it? There are still a couple of things to sort out, but I'm going to leave that to Angeliki. She's over the moon."

"And you're not?"

Rolf laughed: "I would rather stay at home in Kavavdades."

Japan would be very far away ..., thought Sophie and felt a slight dip in her mood, which shocked her. *What is the matter with me?*

"Oh well, we'll see how it all turns out. What will be, will be. I've learned that from experience. Let's get going, otherwise the market will be closed already."

The architecture in the historical centre of Kerkyra, the capital city of the island, reflects its multicultural past and the influence of Italians, French and English. The expansive and most impressive square *Esplanada* is surrounded by countless atmospheric cafés and is the centre point of the night life in town. Here you can experience the stylistic Aristocrats promenade with traditional French flair, a cricket pitch dating back to the British colonial era and elegant Venetian houses in the old part of town, all in close vicinity of each other. In the very obviously Italian influence old town there are numerous exciting alleys, squares, churches and chapels. the atmosphere is very lively.

There is a wonderful view from the *Old* and the *New Fortresses*, which were built to provide safety for the Venetians and the Greeks from possible Turkish invasions. The picturesque alleyways illustrate the many differences between Kerkyra and other Greek towns, for the Turkish architectural influences are missing here. Old windows and balconies with wrought iron railings are reminiscent of Italy and recall the four hundred year-long Venetian colonial era. One of the most beautiful views is to be beheld from the roof of *Hotel Cavalieri*.

First, they strolled through the market at the foot of the Old Fortress, which they reached after a 15-minute walk. They bought the cherries, which both loved so much, and kumquats steeped in honey, then they settled themselves into one of the small cafés.

He had spontaneously taken her by the hand, and she had not rejected the gesture. In the direct vicinity there was a stand selling fresh fish, cockles, octopuses and prawns. This was where the most delicious, sea-salt seasoned sardines and calamari that they had ever eaten, had come from. They told themselves that they would eat there again, the next time they were to visit the town.

Later, they sauntered through the picturesque Old Town with its countless shops and here too Sophie could not see enough of the buildings, the people and the bustle of it all. Whilst they were in one of the small shops collecting a pair of trousers he had ordered a few days ago, the proprietor of the shop could not believe that Sophie wasn't Greek. She constantly tried to speak Greek to her. They left the shop laughing.

"Maybe she had seen something." said Rolf, after they had continued a short way.

"Who do you mean?"

"Back there, the lady in the shop."

"What was she supposed to have seen?"

"That you were once a Greek ... that happens to me all the time, that people keep taking me for a Greek, but I had mentioned that to you already."

"Now listen Rolf, I still find that very difficult to believe. Do you really think we have really seen into past lives?"

"What else was it supposed to be then?"

"I have absolutely no idea either."

"Do you fancy going to see the Achilleion? There's plenty of time until dinner and it is only seven kilometres away."

,,Achilleion?"

"Yes, it is the former palace of the Austrian Empress Elisabeth, the one who was better known as Sissie."

"The one who is loved by every little girl. I've no idea just how often I have seen those films! They used to be on at Christmas time every year."

"They still are."

"I haven't followed the programmes for the last few years. I always had to work on the bank holidays, so that the colleagues with families could have time off. I generally take holiday at new year instead. Then we usually go skiing to Austria, almost always to Arlberg."

As Rolf felt a slight tightening in his chest, he had to admit to himself that he was beginning to fall on love with Sophie.

Leo, you old fox, had been right and he had recognised it even before me. But she is a wonderful woman, he thought.

"If your schedule permits, I would gladly take you up on your offer with the castle." said Sophie.

"I did say that I haven't much on my plate at the moment and I haven't been there for a long time. Afterwards we can still go and eat sushi. But to be on the safe side, I'll go and reserve a table."

"Umm, actually I had arranged to meet up with Martha this evening ... but do you know what? I'll text her and see if it can wait until breakfast time. It is not often that I get the opportunity to walk in the footsteps of an empress, am I right? I'll go sit on the bench over there and do it."

"HELLO MARTHA, I'M SORRY BUT IT IS LIKELY TO BE QUITE LATE AGAIN THIS EVENING.. WE WANT TO GO TO THE ACHILLEION AND AFTERWARDS GO FOR SOMETHING TO EAT. COULD WE POSTPONE OUR CHAT UNTIL TOMORROW MORNING? LOVE FROM SOPHIE"

Meanwhile, Rolf had reserved the table using his phone.

"OK Rolf, we can go, I've written to Martha."

"Great, then let's hope that the queue of tourists at the counter isn't too long. I hate queuing."

"Me too!" laughed Sophie and then she felt her phone vibrating.

"Hang on a minute, I think Martha has answered already."

"HELLO SOPHIE, ALRIGHT, NO PROBLEM AT ALL. JUST COME OVER AT BREAKFAST TIME. WE'LL BE AT HOME ALL MORNING. HAVE A NICE EVENING. LOVE MARTHA ;-)"

The winking smiley, how typical, thought Sophie amusedly and wrote back:

"TOMORROW YOU ARE INVITED TO EAT BREAKFAST AT MINE. ON THE WAY HOME FROM THE BEACH I BOUGHT A COUPLE OF THINGS. BY THE WAY, THE COFFEE-MACHINE IN THE APARTMENT IS PERFECT! THEN WE CAN CHAT IN PEACE. SEE YOU! S"

CHAPTER 10

To make you question yourselves, to make you love yourselves, is all that matters: because that is the one being with whom you must live and feel with. When you begin to do this, you will be free. Free! This enables you to break out of the box and expand your imagination and thoughts. Just imagine that you don't have to worry about how you come across to others or what they think about you. Once this has disappeared from your mindset and you are free of it, can you imagine how you could be? Happy! Happy! (Ramtha)

The *Achilleion* is one of the greatest attractions on the island. Many tour operators include a visit to this former palace in their itinerary and it is advisable to arrive in the early morning. It is not only the interior that is worth seeing, but also the gardens with the countless sculptures, not to mention wonderful view. The famous Empress Elizabeth of Austria herself commissioned the building of this majestic summer palace, after she ordered the demolition of the ancient villa that had previously stood there.

It is a three-storey palace built along classical lines which is surrounded by a large garden containing impressive artwork. The architect of this unique construction was the Italian *Raffaele Carito*.

After the murder of the Empress, Emperor Wilhelm II bought it from her daughters. However, the outbreak of

World War I prevented his further enjoyment of the palace. These days, the Achilleion is a Museum.

In 1884 the Empress had the marble statue entitled *"The Death of Achilles"* erected.

After Kaiser Wilhelm II became the owner, he ordered the replacement of this statue by the erection of a new one, *"Achilles Victorious."* This eleven-metre-tall statue sports a bronze shield and spear. Even today, both statues can still be observed in the palace gardens. In front of the entrance stands a statue of the Empress, which she herself would not have liked. The entire property is furnished with her pictures, artefacts and sculptures related to Greek mythology.

Elisabeth had a great love for antique Greece. She named the Palace after the Greek hero Achilles, whom she admired for his great strength, as well as his divine good looks.

Achilles was the son of Peleus and the sea nymph Thetis. As the offspring of a human father and an immortal mother, he was himself mortal. However, in order to convene invincibility on her son, his mother bathed him in the river Styx, which divides the realms of the living and the underworld. Unfortunately, the place where she held him remained untouched and with it, vulnerable.

Sophie walked in amazement through the surrounds of the former Palace.

"It is wonderful here Rolf, just look at the view of the town."

"All things considered, if money is not an option, you can build places like this, but irrespective of that they didn't scrimp on details, as you can see. It reminds me a little of the White House in Washington ... with all those pillars."

"She was supposedly very happy here. At least that is how it was portrayed in the films ... Oh, look," Sophie pointed to an area in the garden, "It must have been just here where they filmed the famous scene where Sissie is lying on the lounger and ..."

"I'm afraid I have to disappoint you there," Rolf interrupted. "Not a single scene was filmed here. Apparently that would have been too expensive for the film producers. They simply used pictures of Corfu as a backdrop. On the whole the Empress is put across as being fairly stereotyped and actually falsely portrayed."

"She was supposedly a very narcissistic person, not to mention a terrible mother and a sport fanatic. It is said that there was a fitness studio in the palace in Vienna and that she reputedly exercised for up to ten hours a day. In any case, she was supposed to have been completely over her head in her role as Empress, which for a sixteen-year-old is not surprising. The most important day in her life was almost certainly the day she was crowned queen of Hungary."

"And how do you know all that?"

"As you are aware, I read quite a lot." laughed Rolf

"Well, I wonder whether the countless fans who come here to visit are aware of all that?"

"I very much doubt it, but let's leave them to their illusions, at least here they are walking in the footsteps of the real Sissie. Although it is a shame that her daughters removed the larger part of the furniture. They have used it to furnish their own palaces. Word has it that the Greek food did not entirely agree with her. She followed a strict diet and apart from wine had everything imported in from Vienna. She was supposed to have like the wine though, as she did cocaine. Incidentally her husband never set foot on the island."

Rolf laughed again and Sophie found herself liking his laugh very much.

"She took cocaine? Really?"

"Yes, it was recommended to her as a remedy against melancholy. If you were to do that it would be the end of your career, wouldn't it?" he grinned.

"You can bet your boots on that! ... Although it most probably helped her."

"I can completely understand why she suffered from depression, looking at the life she had been forced into. 'Delivered' is how she described it, that after her death she would escape through a tiny hole to fly to freedom and that is exactly what happened. The wound from the arrow that hit her in the back and penetrated her heart was said to be only eight millimetres in diameter."

"Sounds very prophetical."

"At one time the castle was even a casino, I can remember it, because I was here a couple of times ... and in 1980 it was one of the locations in the *James Bond* film '*For your eyes only*.' Roger Moore sits and has dinner on the garden terrace. Have you seen the film?"

"Yes, I do ... though I must admit Sean Connery is the only one true *James Bond* in my book."

84

"For me too ... Maybe because he was the very first Bond actor that I saw. I am conditioned towards him, if you like." smiled Rolf.

He checked the time.

"Well, we'd better get going. I reserved the table for seven o'clock."

CHAPTER 11

You are part of another "YOU," whose calling is an excellent adventure called LIFE - it is to be investigated, to be learned from and to achieve something from. Your souls and your spirit share with each other. You move as one in and out of experiences. What you feel at this moment, the other feels also. What you recognise today as understanding and openness the other recognises as clairvoyant visions. (Ramtha)

Wednesday

Sophie had set the breakfast out on the terrace table with care. There was freshly squeezed orange juice, fig marmalade, cheese and boiled eggs. Not forgetting the obligatory the Greek yoghurt of course! She had been up and out early on her motor scooter and bought fresh bread and chocolate croissants.

"Good morning Sophie!" said Martha jovially as she joined her. "Thank you very much for the invitation! I can see you have thought of everything, it looks delicious. You must have been to Kostas Avgerinos bakery; he has been delivering many of the restaurants and hotels around here for years. And up until recently with an old banger that must have been at least thirty years old, according to Kostas! His daughter Maria usually works behind the counter."

"Oh, I didn't know she was called Maria too. In any case, she was very friendly. Do take a seat, I'll just go and get the coffee ... or would you prefer a Greek mountain tea? I discovered it yesterday in the super-market, it smelled divine. I haven't tried it yet though."

"No thanks, I'd rather have a coffee. The mountain tea is quite good, lots of people take it back home to Germany with them."

Sophie came back a moment later with the coffee."

"I'm almost bursting with curiosity, Sophie!" Martha blurted out, after a sip of her coffee. "Come on, tell me all about it, how was your day?"

"The sushi was really delicious ..."

Martha interrupted her: "The sushi, yes, I know, but that is not what I mean, and you know that very well!"

Sophie laughed. "Yes, I know, nosy!"

She spent the next hour telling her friend everything: From her experience on the bench at Afionas, after their meal at the *Three Brothers*; that which Rolf had seen in his vision; to the day they spent together in town. She omitted nothing.

Silence reigned for a while afterwards.

"That is, like, unbelievable!" exclaimed Martha.

"Yes, that's exactly what I thought too and to tell you the truth, I still find it very hard to believe it all."

"What now?"

"What do you mean, 'what now?' I have absolutely no idea. In any case, I've never felt so familiar with any-one in such a short time before, as I do with Rolf."

"So why are you crying?"

Martha had not missed seeing her tears.

"I don't know, I'm ... confused ... Well, I've no idea how I should put it. My life in Germany is so well sorted out ... and then I come here and after two days, this. All my defence mechanisms have suddenly failed me."

"I can understand that, Sophie."

"Really?"

"Yes, because it's not the first time I've heard it. This place seems to awaken things ... I don't know how I should put it. It must be the islands energy. Participants of the seminars tell me that all the time. Since I've been living here, my dreams are far more intense, so much more realistic and livelier than they ever were in Germany."

"Same here, just think back to my first night here."

"But it's actually quite obvious why this is happening."

"Why?"

"Well, think about your life in Muenster. nothing but hectic. There's not much time to sit back and consider the important things in life. Here you have time to switch off, and so some of the things that were permanently buried under at home, have a chance to break the surface. That's how I see it, anyway."

"Maybe you're right."

"Of course I am, believe me. And? What do you think about your visions? I mean you weren't exactly dreaming in the normal sense. You said that you weren't asleep while you were sitting on the bench in Afionas."

"Yes, that's right, I was awake ... very awake indeed and Rolf was standing on the terrace too, whilst he was having his. So he couldn't have been asleep."

"Can you still remember what we had spoken about, before?"

"You mean our conversation about reincarnation?"

"Yes, that's the one, I mean, you vehemently rejected that train of thought."

"I had the same conversation with Rolf too, when I met him in Ammos. He believes in it."

"Like most of the people on this planet."

"I know!"

"Maybe it doesn't matter whether you believe in it or not."

Deep down inside, Sophie wasn't so sure anymore, but she fought off the little voice, that she was now hearing for the second time.

"Possibly."

Sophie's mobile buzzed.

"One moment, a WhatsApp."

"HELLO SOPHIE, COULDN'T GET THROUGH TO YOU YESTERDAY. SO NOW TRYING TO GET YOU IN THE MORNING. HOW ARE YOU? PLEASE GET IN TOUCH, KISS, MICHAEL."

"From Rolf?"

"No, ... From Michael, I think he's worried. I had forgotten to switch my phone back on. When we went for sushi I'd switched it off."

"Should he be worried?"

"No, he shouldn't. This is just purely my thing and it is going to stay here."

"Well, OK, if that's what you want."

"Yes, I mean it, Martha. I'll call him back later."

"What does Michael do for a living? You've never mentioned it."

"He's a software developer. Can you remember, two years ago I mentioned that we were getting a new IT system? We now use iPad and the like. It has the advantage that we always have the patients' records to hand when we do the ward rounds. We met during the software presentation. The company was based in Bremen and because his colleague there was ill and Michael had time off, he was able to fill in for him. One of your famous coincidences, don't you think?"

"Yes, exactly! And what are you going to do today? You and Rolf, I mean."

"I am going to the beach today. I need some time to myself. But tomorrow Rolf wants to show me an old mountain village."

"Well, that's enough for now, Martha, thank you for listening, it helped immensely. I'm going to go and pack my things together, swing on to my bike and ride to the beach. I'm going to look for a different spot today, over in St. Stefanos. The beach looked larger than the one in Arillas."

"It is too. Although I only go there when I take Maria with me, because the water is shallow. You have to go quite a way out, before you can swim. It's ideal for children. In any case, you will find several good taverns there. Further along you can even bathe nude, but you can do that in Arillas too, if you go far to the right, but you'll see that when you get there."

"I'm sure I'll find a good spot. I need some peace and quiet, that's for sure ... and I'm not planning on skinny dipping!"

"You'll probably be going up the Pantokrator then tomorrow. There is an old deserted village there. Well, it's not quite so deserted anymore, but I don't want to spoil the surprise, it is very beautiful. I went there with Kostas during my first visit here too. It is the highest mountain on the island, nearly a thousand metres."

CHAPTER 12

Well then, what is God's voice? What is this knowledge that you believe will come down from heaven like a lightning bolt to tell you what you should do? Feelings is what it is. God's words are feelings. To listen to God's voice implies that you are listening to your emotions. Feelings are really the incommunicable knowledge. Can you now understand why I cannot teach you this knowledge because you are the ones who must feel it! I can tell you about the emotion, but you will never understand what I am saying until you have experienced the feeling for yourselves. Do you understand now? (Ramtha)

Sophie walked along a stretch of beach, enjoying the light breeze that was blowing over from the Albanian mountains. The waves were rolling gently in and somewhere children were shouting, a small group of pensioners were playing bowls. After ten minutes she found a spot and unrolled her beach towel. Not far away a couple were up to their knees in water, playing beach tennis. She set out her book, '*Prospero's cell,*' ready to read later.

But first, time for a quick dip, she thought and ran into the water. It was cold, but after a couple of strong strokes she had got used to the temperature.

This is doing me the world of good, I'll answer Michael back in a bit.

A quarter of an hour later, she dried herself off and changed her bathing suit. She lay herself down and picked up her mobile.

"HELLO LOVE, I'M AT THE BEACH, IT IS WONDER-FUL. I ACTUALLY WANTED TO LEAVE MY MOBILE AT HOME, BUT I JUST HAD TO WRITE BACK TO YOU. YESTERDAY I FORGOT TO SWITCH IT BACK ON, I'M SORRY. HOW ARE YOU? I WOULD HAVE LOVED TO HAVE A CHAT, BUT I KNOW YOU CAN'T BECAUSE YOU ARE AT WORK. WE'LL SPEAK THIS EVENING OK? BIG KISS, S"

Then she took the book and leafed through it with her eyes closed and opened it randomly. Last year she had been to a party and friends of hers had said that when you do that, what was then written there was supposed to have a significant meaning, like Tarot cards. She had taken this for superstitious nonsense, but now she thought she would give it a try.

"The island is really the saint: and the saint is the island. Nearly all the male children are named after him. All the island craft carry his tintype - mournful of beard and brow - nailed to their masts of unseasoned cypress wood. To use his name in an oath is to bind yourself by the most solemn of vows, for St. Spiridon is still awake in Corfu after nearly two thousand years on earth. He is the influence on the island.

In the chapel of the church of his name he lies, looking a trifle misanthropic but determined, as befits one who has seen both sides of life on earth, and who is on equal terms with heaven. The sarcophagus is deeply lined and comfortable; he lies in hibernating stillness in his richly wrought casket, whose outer shell of silver is permanently clouded by the breath of the faithful who stoop to kiss it."

After reading a couple of pages Sophie felt sleepy and put the book to one side.

When we go to town I would like to visit this church, she thought. Meanwhile it had become quite warn and she closed her eyes. The monotonic sound of the ball hitting the racquets combined with the gentle swell of the tide had a relaxing, hypnotic effect.

The coach jolts along slowly over the path to Kassiopi. Her mother Melania and old accompany her. Her father's oldest and most f͟a͟ servant Petros is driving the drenched coach h͟o͟r͟s͟e͟s͟ with a steady hand. Just after their departure there had been a short but heavy downpour. Now as the sun had chased the clouds from the sky, white steam is rising up from the animals' backs. The three women inside the coach are wrapped up in thick woollen blankets, since it is cold on this late December day. This time Helena has no interest in watching the beautiful, native countryside pass by. The wooden signpost showing the way to town comes into view and Petros whips the horses up into a gentle trot. There was no one to be seen on the way, for those who could, stayed at home on a day such as this.

Her father, the rich businessman and landowner, Angelos Pachis, is the only person near and far to own horses and he had brought the coach over on one of his own ships from Venice.

"Stop crying, child" chastens her mother, "It is no use. Your father only wants the best for you. You should be thankful that you will soon be meeting your future husband, after all, you are already sixteen years old."

Helena sobs bitterly.

"Do you want to spend the rest of your life in a dilapidated hut ... with a husband who can't even afford to care for himself? You don't think that I haven't noticed you stealing food from the pantry to take to him. You should be glad that I haven't informed your father ... I dread to think what he would do if he knew."

"Me neither," cackles the old servant maid, who, on the orders of her father has been following her every step of late. She has noticed this of course and is secretly overjoyed when the old woman can't manage to follow her to their secret trysts. It is too far up and only accessible via steep paths. Full of woe, she thinks about the many hours she has spent with Nikos under the gnarled olive tree. In the arms of her lover she could forget everything.

She sobs again, miserably. Not because of the journey to Kerkyra, but because of the secret she carries within her. For three weeks now, she knows that she is with child, Nikos child. It is not yet visible, but she will not be able to hide it for much longer. Then her father will not hesitate to send her to a convent on the mainland.

There is one good thing about the trip to town though, she will light a candle to saint Spyridon, kiss his slippers and beg him for assistance. He did save the island from the plague after all. So their pleas will surely be a simple matter for him.

Sophie opened her eyes with a start and sat up. The beach scene was just as peaceful as it had been before, just the couple playing tennis had gone. She involuntarily burst into tears.

Damn it! What is the matter with me? I'll go insane if this carries on much longer, she thought, horrified, *why am I reacting liking this? Then perhaps it wasn't just esoteric rubbish with the book. I must investigate the saint of the island. I'll have to ask Rolf if we could go back to town, I simply must go there.*

She reached for her water bottle and drank from it thirstily. Then she stood up, ran to the sea and dived in. After submerging herself a couple of times she went for a short walk along the beach. Holidaymakers were lounging all around, enjoying the good weather. Some of them even had sunburn already. A motorboat was pulling a paraglider along behind it.

She checked her watch and realised that it was already midday.

I'll go and have something to eat, that will take my mind off things.

She looked around and spotted at beach bar with large white sunshades, that seemed to belong to an hotel called *Delfino Blu.*

She managed to get hold of the last vacant table and a friendly waiter brought her the menu. She chose Linguini and ordered a Cola light to go with it. She picked up her mobile to take a couple of photos and at that moment it vibrated.

"HELLO, SOPHIE, JUST STOPPED FOR MY LUNCH BREAK AND WAS THINKING OF YOU. HOW ARE YOU? HAVE YOU GOT SUNBURN ALREADY? I CAN'T WAIT FOR YOU TO COME HOME, EVEN THOUGH YOU REALLY DESERVE YOUR HOLIDAY, SEND ME A COUPLE OF PHOTOS! NEXT TIME WE'LL GO ON HOLIDAY TOGETHER. LOOKING FORWARD TO SPEAKING TO YOU THIS EVENING, LOVE AND HUGS, MICHAEL."

Usually Sophie answered Michael immediately.

I can't answer him now, she thought. *What am I supposed to tell him? That I'm looking forward to seeing him too? I feel so distant from him at the moment ... I really must be honest, and particularly with myself. But I will call him this evening.*

Just then, the waiter brought her Coke.

"Your Linguini will be ready shortly." he said.

CHAPTER 13

You see, many of you have lost yourselves to the ideals dictated by society - a beautiful appearance, standards of living, wealth, acclaim, power. Those are your blockades, the summation of your dreams. You want to be beautiful, desirable. You want to be the most famous. And you want to be powerful, to be "on the ball." You want to be these things because they raise you up above the usual monotony in life. But you are living in a box! (Ramtha)

Whilst Sophie was eating her Linguini, Rolf was standing in front of the car wash salon in Sidari and watched his old Jeep with the licence plate KYM-8864 being cleaned, both inside and out.

The young man who was doing such a thorough job on it was getting splashed a lot whilst working. Afterwards Rolf opened the roof up again and climbed into the now shining Jeep. He inhaled the smell of the interior, took a CD of Irene Papas, a Greek singer, out of the glove compartment and inserted it into the player. After he had split up from Susanne he had wanted to throw the CD away, because it had been her favourite music. Fortunately, he had managed to resist that childish impulse.

With *'Oh, my Sweet Springtime'* in the air he drove back to Arillas to eat something at Graziella. He loved the terrace that was right next to the beach. He had been friends with the owners Aristides and Kostas for a long time now. He had even made the acquaintance of their father Thomaso who used to greet the guests while he ate, sitting on the stairs which lead down the beach. He had served in Italy during the war and was able to speak a little Italian, so when Italian guests came by he beamed from ear to ear, pleased that he had someone to converse with.

Rolf took his laptop out. He urgently needed to write a few emails to two gallery managers in Germany and recount the story of his dealings in Japan to his sister, who was five years his senior. She would certainly be very pleased about it for him. She was one of the few people previously, who had supported his decision to give up the architecture for photography. His father had not forgiven her for a very long time.

Aristides came to the table.

"Rolf, I have a wonderful sea bream for you, caught first thing this morning, how about it?"

"Oh, yes that sounds perfect ... but since I had tomatoes with feta cheese and Tzatziki earlier ... I'll take the Bream without the side servings ... and a glass of white wine."

As he had expected, the fish tasted superb and he savoured the lightly resinated cold wine.

"So, did it fulfill expectations?" queried Aristides when he came to clear the table.

"Yes, you are always right about the fish, my friend."

"Do you see the lads over there?" Aristides jerked his head in the direction of some young people who were very noticeably different from the other guests due to their clothes and hair styles.

"Yes, what's the matter with them?"

"They have only ordered a glass of water and have been blocking that table for over an hour.

"They haven't eaten anything?"

Aristides smiled. "Oh yes, their own sandwiches."

"And you let them?"

"What can I do? I don't want any trouble."

"Does that happen often?"

"On a daily basis, when they hold their festivals. One started three days ago. But then again, I'm not the only proprietor to be upset about it."

"Maybe they haven't got enough money."

Aristides laughed. "Do you know what it costs?"

"No, I'm not interested in that sort of thing, I never really went to church. If I want to hear a good mantra concert I go to Satya and Pari in Zorbas or to Ouranos."

"And to top it all, there's the loud music as well," added Aristides, "The guests in the hotels over there can hardly sleep a wink at night, but it doesn't bother them at all."

Not long after, Rolf closed his laptop and paid the young waiter for his bill. They all seemed to belong to the family here!

On doing so, he remembered that twenty years ago the meal cost only five Marks and that was for two people. For his meagre student allowance, it just about worked out. Now it cost four times as much for just the one person, and that was still relatively moderate, as he well knew.

Rolf retrieved his bathing things out of the car, he always had a set with him, just in case, ran down the stairs to the beach and turned left.

A little later he arrived at his favourite spot. There weren't many bathers there and they were far enough away not to disturb a midday nap. The sea had washed reeds ashore and they had piled up high. The top layers had been dried off by the sun during the last couple of days, so he spread out his beach towel with the Greek flag design and laid himself down on it. *Like on a feather bed* he thought, *How divine. Now just a short nap to digest the fish.*

"Nikos, my dear, you have to get to school, hurry up!" His mother is standing in the doorway to his room and has her hands on her hips. Over her long dress that had presumably once been blue, she wears an already worn out apron. This is now covered in dark stains and he assumes his mother has already been stacking wood early that morning. Agra, the big white dog who is expecting a litter of puppies comes up to him and licks his face with her rough tongue.

"Oh, Mum, I was in the middle of such a lovely dream, let me sleep. It's boring at school anyway, I know everything already and you, Agra, I can wash my own face," he laughs. "You'll be in trouble if you don't have a healthy litter, I can tell you, because one of them is for me."

"You little know-it-all," laughs Medeia and a considerable gap in her teeth shows in her from hard work and from the elements, weathered face. Despite her young years she looks nearly forty years old. Everyone says he has inherited her magnificent black hair.

"You want to be careful what you say at your age," she says wryly, "if could get you into trouble, that mouth of yours. And you'll be getting a pup from the next litter. Then you will have time to look after it. Right now, it's time for school."

"Why though, I'm the best at reading, even better than the oldest in the class and they are already fourteen. our Pope has even given me a book by Homer, I can read to you out of it."

He knows that she hadn't been able to go to school, but that doesn't bother him, she's the best mother in the world to him.

"I know that. I would love you to, I love listening to stories," she says, "But now it is time to get out of bed, get washed and dressed. Breakfast is in the kitchen, I have to go working in the fields. And if you don't go to school, you'll be in big trouble, I can tell you!"

He doesn't want to push it too far, so he throws back the heavy woollen blanket that always felt a little damp. His eyes wander over to the empty bed on the other side of the room. Ekaterina his little sister had not survived the fever from the year before. Sighing, he stands up and goes outside to the well. He lets the bucket down and pours the icy cold water over himself. He immediately breaks out in goose flesh, for even though it is June it is still quite cool so early in the morning up in the mountains. He dries himself off with a large linen cloth full of holes and looks up. There on the peak of the Pantokrator was the monastery he wants to visit that afternoon, as long as his father doesn't get hold of him to herd the sheep.

He loves talking to the monks. Angelos has even taught him a little Latin. If his father notices that, he will be beaten but he was willing to take the risk. He finally knows what he wants to be later. A priest ... a few bruises, that will be gone a few days later, are a small price to pay for that. The little Helena who had joined the school six months ago, had teased him about it a few days back.

"Has your father been beating you again? What did you do this time?" But he had ignored her and even spat out in front of her. Then he had turned on his heel and gone on his way, shaking his head.

The spoilt brat, he had thought.

He goes back into the house and looks through his clothes box. There isn't much choice, but once he is a priest he will wear magnificent vestments. Lost in thought, he spoons up the barley porridge and drinks a glass of fresh goat's milk, just like every morning. Then he grabs the goat-skin satchel that his grandfather had given him on his last name-day and leaves the small stone cottage. Soon he will have to stoop to go through the front door. He picks a handful of cherries from the tree to go with the wedge of bread that would have to suffice for the rest of the day. During the fifteen-minute walk to school, he imagines how he will later sit before a wonderful spread provided by the community on the feast days. There will be black coffee, sausage, cake and red wine. Perhaps one day he will be bishop of Kerkyra, you never know.

Rolf opened his eyes and just had to laugh out loud. A young couple who were running past glanced around in interest.

"Probably one of the seminar participants," suggested the man to his companion, who grinned in response.

"Probably from the Samarpan-Group."

The pair of them ran on, sniggering.

"Little Helena, the beast. Well, plenty has changed in Nikos life," he murmured.

Then he ran into the water.

Late in the afternoon, he had fallen into a deep and dreamless sleep after the swimming, he drove back to his house which was in the vicinity of the restaurant *Mon Amour* in Kavadades. He brewed himself a tea and sat with it on his terrace. He would never get bored of the view he had from there. It looked over a green valley made up of Olive trees, bamboo and Cypresses and far out over the sea by Arillas to the island Mathraki and every sunset was magical. Sometimes a Greek neighbour would drive her goats and sheep back through the valley to their stalls, always singing the same songs and those were the moments when he realised that he had been exactly right in his decision to move there. He often thanked his grandfather silently for the inheritance he had bequeathed him some time ago, which had enabled him to purchase the house.

He picked up his mobile phone.

"HELLO SOPHIE, HOW ARE YOU? I HAVE SOMETHING TO TELL YOU - IT'S COMPLETELY INSANE. ARE YOU STILL ON FOR OUR TRIP TOMORROW? I'M LOOKING FORWARD TO IT. LOVE FROM, ROLF"

At the same moment Sophie was in the hammock behind her apartment. The sun was still agreeably warm, and she was reading the book that Rolf had given her.

That must have been some life they had, she had just thought to herself.

"HI ROLF, I WANTED TO WRITE TO YOU LATER TOO, BECAUSE I HAVE SOMETHING TO TELL YOU TOO. YES, EVERYTHING IS FINE FOR TOMORROW, I'M LOOKING FORWARD TO GOING TO THE VILLAGE. HAVE A NICE EVENING. I'LL BE GOING TO BED EARLY THIS EVENING AS I AM SO TIRED. A BEACH DAY IS SO STRENUOUS! :-) :-) LOVE FROM SOPHIE."

"I've brought you a coffee, Sophie, and you really must try one of these chocolates, look here."

Martha held out a cup and a plate to her.

"Oh, that is very good of you, can you read minds? I really fancied a coffee just now. Wait up, let me get out, otherwise there will be a catastrophe."

"Then let's go on to the terrace. Unbelievable how tanned you are already ... in such a short time, look at me!"

Sophie laughed: "I always go brown very quickly. A dark complexion, you know."

And the English are probably all lying out there looking like lobsters." laughed Martha out loud.

"Some are, yes."

"Then you had better go to Sidari, they wander around there in hordes, and with ugly tattoos to boot."

"Sidari?"

"Yes it is a place not far from here ... really ugly, if you ask me ... but with a beautiful beach and loads of pubs. Probably not your thing ... although ..."

"Although what?"

"You should take a look at Canal A'mour once." grinned Martha.

"Don't start that again!"

"Oh, for goodness sake!"

"OK, I will ... and do you know what? I will take a look at this Canal, next time I come with Michael."

"Oh, come on, don't be so sensitive. Tell me what you got up to today. Did you have another vision and where did you have lunch? I'm sorry, it won't happen again."

"It's alright," smiled Sophie, "I forgive you. I am far too thankful that you let me stay here with you. And yes, I did have another vision. I get the feeling I am being stalked by them. It is very strenuous."

Sophie told her friend about her experience at the beach and she listened in amazement, without interrupting once.

"Unbelieeevable!" was all she could say.

"Yes, you could put it that way. I don't know what it means, but I can't stop it happening to me."

"Why in earth should you? I wish I had had such an experience ... and what did you do later? Have you already told Rolf about it?

"No, I'm going to tell him about it tomorrow. Afterwards I ate on the terrace of the Delfino Blu Hotel and it was delicious."

"We wanted to go there with you on your last evening ... as a grand finale, so to speak."

"Oh, don't talk to me of my last evening already!"

"If you want to stay longer you can, but whatever happens you must come again soon. You have to promise me, not to wait another five years before coming again!"

"Usually I'm pretty reluctant to make promises, but I'm willing to make that one!"

"Well I shall be sure I remind you ... right, I'd better get going, Kostas wants to go into town to purchase something and Maria insisted on going with him ... so we are all going to go. Oh yes, our tomcat is back, you have a nice evening ... and a lovely day tomorrow."

"Thank you very much, I'll be going to bed early, so that I am fit for it."

In the club this evening is a Mantra concert, go and see it, I'm sure you will like it. It starts at seven o'clock up in the seminar room in Gravia. If I had time I would go there ... or shall we go to the next one together, what do you think?"

"That's a good idea, let's do that. Say hello to Kostas and Maria from me."

CHAPTER 14

Where is your soul mate right now? There are some of you whose soul mate is at this moment on this same plane. There are others, whose soul mate at this moment is on another plane or in a different universe. Do you know what connects the two of you? Feelings! You are so close to each other. So close. (Ramtha)

Thursday

Sophie didn't need an alarm clock. A dog that was barking right in front of the open terrace door gave her a rude awakening. She glanced at her watch which was lying on the bedside table.

"Bello, how do you know what time I have to get up?" she murmured, half asleep.

Then she switched off the flight mode and checked the weather App.

Sun, Sun, Sun, she thought, *and up to twenty-eight degrees, super. Oh, a message from Michael. Damn! I've completely forgotten to call him.*

"HELLO SOPHIE, YOU HAD PROMISED TO CALL ME BACK. THAT'S NOT LIKE YOU. WHAT'S THE MATTER? I'M BEGINNING TO GET A LITTLE WORRIED. ARE YOU REALLY ALRIGHT? I STAYED UP UNTIL MIDNIGHT WAITING FOR YOUR CALL. TRIED TO GET IN TOUCH LOADS OF TIMES. COULD HARDLY SLEEP. OUT AND ABOUT ALL DAY WITH CLIENTS. PLEASE CALL ME THIS EVENING, NO MATTER WHAT. LOVE, FROM MICHAEL."

"Shit," she uttered, "Now look what I have done, now he's angry ... OK. Can't do anything about it now ... well it'll be an interesting chat this evening."

"HELLO MICHAEL, I'M SO SORRY. I WENT TO BED REALLY EARLY LAST NIGHT, HAD A STRENUOUS DAY. LEFT THE PHONE IN FLIGHT MODE. SHALL DEFINITELY CALL YOU BACK THIS EVENING. NO NEED TO WORRY, EVERYTHING IS FINE HERE. GOOD LUCK WITH YOUR CLIENTS. BIG KISS, S."

She got up and after she put the coffee machine on, went to have a shower. She dressed in lightweight, widely cut, white trousers and white trainers.

That's a pain, I've only got one clean shirt left and of all colours it has to be white. Oh well, then white it is.

She sat herself down with her coffee outside on the terrace

I've got a couple of minutes yet.

A moment later a car horn sounded.

Punctual as clockwork, she grinned. On her way out she reached for her bag and a thin cardigan.

Rolf was standing next to his Jeep.

"Oh, Doctor, I'm afraid to inform you that I am not insured."

Sophie laughed and climbed in.

"You have no insurance, Mr. Wendtland? That is very naive of you ... ...no, seriously, don't you have any health insurance?

"No, I haven't."

"Why ever not?"

"I trust in life ... and if I ever need treatment, like, at the dentist, I pay up front."

"Well, if you can afford it "

111

"Then just think what a private insurance costs per year, that's an awful lot of money. At least seven thousand Euros."

"Yes, that's right, but then I hope that you'll never need a major operation, let's talk about something else."

"Before we set off, there's another thing."

He passed her a blue baseball cap.

"Protection against the draught, or shall I put the roof back up ... or so that you don't completely look like a doctor."

"Thanks, fits in with your car well, green and blue. Please leave the roof down. You had it washed, didn't you?"

"Yes, yesterday. But you were going to tell me something."

"Yes, but you did too, so who is going to start?"

"You," he said, "Shall I put the radio on?"

"'Course."

"Oh, who is the singer, the song is lovely!"

They were listening to the song *Little Orange Tree*.

"She's called Irene Papas."

"I've never heard of her."

"Do you know the film Alexis Sorbas? The one with Anthony Quinn? She played the widow Surmelina."

"Oh, really? Yes, I know the film ... although 'The Hunchback of Notre Dame' and 'The Old Man and the Sea' are my favourite films of his.

"Mine are 'A Walk in the Clouds,' in which he plays a winegrower and 'Laurence of Arabia.' I think he has played in over eighty films and he was nominated for an Oscar for his role of Alexis."

"How do you know all this?"

"As you know ..."

"... you read a lot," interrupted Sophie, smiling, "Yes I've heard!"

The song *Menoussis* was playing.

"That is a really good CD that you have there. Can you buy it here?"

"I'm pretty sure you can, but don't you have Spotify? These Irene Papas songs were Susanne's favourites. After we split up I almost threw the CD away in a childish tantrum."

"You wanted to do something like that? Well, aren't I lucky that you didn't do it!"

"Yes, that would have pretty childish, eh?"

"Well, I don't know. Adults sometimes do childish things. I have Spotify. I'll download Irene this evening. SO ... are you going to tell me about the vision you had yesterday? You had one didn't you?"

"That's right ... and you did too?"

On reaching *Avliotes* both had heard what the other had experienced. Then there was silence, both contemplating the revelations.

"Oh look, on the left over there is an ice cream parlour," Sophie called out suddenly, "Do you like ice cream?"

"I love ice cream; we can eat one later if you like. We're nearly at the village, we turn off here and then we go up the mountain."

He was glad the light-heartedness had returned.

The old Venetian village *Paleo Perithia* is another popular place for a day out on the island. Nowadays there are four taverns and a souvenir shop offers the usual trinkets. Despite being quite busy in the main holiday period, a short hike enables one to get the spirit of the area as it might have been long ago.

In the early morning you almost have the village to yourself. Then from about midday onwards the tourists arrive to sit in the taverns or to saunter around the venerable surroundings and ruined buildings. During the evening it gets quieter. In the oldest tavern you can enjoy rabbit stew or higher up near the beehives simply absorb the tranquillity of the place. The beekeeper is always good for a gossip and is generous with the ouzo. If he is in a particularly good mood, you might receive a delicious piece of honeycomb.

Five hundred years ago *Paleo Perithia* was the main town of the *Kassiopi* community with its picturesque harbour and was very wealthy. Most of the houses were built between the fifteenth and seventeenth centuries.

After the end of piracy and a lessening of the dangers of Malaria, people had returned to the coastal regions. It was only towards the middle of the twentieth century that the place became a *ghost village*.

Hand in hand, they sauntered through the old village and spent more than two hours exploring every corner of the place.

"What an idyllic place," said Sophie at once, "It must be lovely to live here, preferably up over there perhaps, where the beautifully renovated houses are."

"Although it is a long way to the sea, but I could imagine living here in the short term. I can show you the pictures I took here a few years ago if you like."

He has had the feeling that he has lived in *Paleo Perithia* before for several years now. In a moment of déjà-vu he even believed that he had found his previous family home at the edge of the village. A dilapidated ruin, now home to scorpions and lizards. He had had a feeling of unknown woefulness. He had sat on one of the remaining steps for a long time.

He mentioned none of this to Sophie.

He checked his watch.

"I know it is only twelve o'clock, but I am quite hungry. You didn't have any breakfast either, did you?"

"No, I didn't. I could do with something to eat."

"Come on then, let's go."

They found a vacant table under a roof of vines at the *Old Perithia* tavern, for a loud group of tourists had occupied almost the entire restaurant. The road to the village had been reconstructed so that there was no access problem, even for long distance coaches.

This had not always been the case. Many years ago, when he came up the Pantokrator, he had needed more than two hours for the journey. Centimetre by centimetre he had cajoled his car up the stony road. He simply had to reach this place, he had no idea why though, then. He finally made it up to the small square in front of the then only tavern that an old married couple had run. He told her about it as they shared a portion of Pastitsio. By then the tourist group had left the pub.

"It is wonderful here, so peaceful. and the food tastes very good."

"You must try the walnut cake too, they are famous for it here."

"Thank you for taking the time to drive me up here."

They were quiet for most of the meal. The villages energy had mesmerized Sophie. The waiter brought the honey-soaked cake and two cups of terrible coffee.

"You were quite right," she laughed, "At least about the cake."

He liked her laugh.

Shortly afterwards they set off again. Slowly they went up the narrow path, which was paved with smooth round flagstones, that so many people had trodden before them. Few had probably previously experienced, that which was due to happen next. He had gone on ahead slightly and had remained standing at the entrance to one of the ruins. The outside walls were still standing, but only half the roof was left. Two stone steps lead into the house. The interior was visible. The floor was ripped up in places and in one corner you could make out where a fireplace had formerly been. He turned around towards her. She was standing there, clutching her chest. She was short of breath and there were tears in her eyes.

"What is the matter?" he asked, worried.

"I don't know, I feel very funny."

"Come here, we'll sit down for a moment."

They sat down on the top step and held hands. They closed their eyes.

"Come on Helena, Spiros says the key is under the second step ... we can stay as long as we want. He won't be coming back until tomorrow. He wants to sell a couple of goats at the market in Agros."

"Then at last we shall finally have time for ourselves, my love. My father is in Kassiopi. His ship sets sail in the evening and he wants to check up on everything. The last time they set off for Venice all the barrels tipped over because the captain hadn't secured them properly. Almost the all the valuable oil was lost in the storm ... and mother is in Afionas, she is helping Yaya with the sheep shearing."

"I'm sorry Helena, but in this case, it is not exactly affecting the impoverished! Your father is the richest man here in the north ... that is why he will never agree to a marriage" he adds morosely.

"Let's worry about that tomorrow my love, let us enjoy the time we have together now."

"How did you get away from that old witch Lamia?"

"She had to go to Afionas with mother, to help with the shearing," she laughs and continues, "Yaya won't like that at all, she hates the old lady ... and she will make her notice it too ... she will probably have to eat in the yard with the dogs."

"She deserves it then."

They run hand in hand up the narrow-flagged path to Spiros house. Today fate is kind to them for there is no-one around in the village to see them. They can hear the regular tapping of the hammer resounding from Konstantinos workshop where the old stonemason works. At the other end of the village a donkey is braying and the bells of the sheep and the goats echo from the steep meadows.

"Hurry, hurry!" he calls to speed her up, "We're lucky there is no one around to betray us."

"I think today I wouldn't care at all!" she answers breathlessly.

"Spiros says we should light a fire in the fireplace, otherwise it could be too cold." he grins cheekily at her, as they stand in front of the house.

He pulls the iron key out from its hiding place under the stone, scaring an emerald green lizard as he does so and inserts it with a shaky hand into the lock.

They enter the little two-roomed stone cottage. The larger living room with the small cooking area and the chimney in the right-hand corner at the rear. A rough wooden table stands in the middle of the room sur-rounded by four chairs, a shelf full of books and a large painted chest.

A low door leads into his friend's small bedroom. The weak twilight filters through the murky window. Out-side an owl hoots its monotonous call. They stand still.

"Oh, listen to the night owl, how I love his song."

"He's searching for a mate." he smiles and takes her by the hand.

"Hey look, he has even given us a bottle of wine. He hardly has enough for himself. I think he would do anything for us."

"Yes, and all his sheepskins are all laid out in front of the fire ... look! Will you read to me later?"

"Yes of course, I nearly always do anyway. What shall I read to you this time, Agapi mou?"

"About the Trojan war ... Helena must have very beautiful if they waged a war just because of her."

He laughs. "You must know Homer's Odyssey off by heart by now, the amount of times that I have read it to you!"

"So many men had vied for her hand," she whispers.

"Yes, and the cunning Odysseus advised her father Tyndareus to make all the suitors swear allegiance to the chosen one in the event of future attacks."

"That is why the army was so large ... all because of a beautiful woman ..."

"She was most certainly not as beautiful as you ... I would challenge the world if it meant I had a chance at winning your hand."

"Idiot!" she laughs and elbows him lovingly in the side, "You won me already, ages ago. Pour me a glass of wine!"

A short while later a crackling fire is burning in the grate, Spiros had provided plenty of wood for it. His faithful friend with whom he shared his secret love would sooner have his tongue cut out rather than betray the lovers.

They stand in a close embrace in front of the fire, completely lost in their own world, not wanting to let go. He inhales the sweet scent of her hair; she pulls him closer towards her.

"Never let me go Nikos, promise me."

They make love on the sheepskin rugs before the fire. Her hair spread out like a veil around her head. He buried his head between her breasts, and she grasps the nape of his neck.....

"My love, please don't stop," she whispers. "Never, my love, never. Keep me in your memory like this ... forever!"

"How could I ever possibly forget you?"

The candles have burned down to their stumps, the olive wood glows, softly crackling in the fireplace and issues a soft light that illuminates her naked body so that it looks almost unreal. Their breathing is relaxed and content in the rhythm of their love. The world outside ceases to exist, they are alone.

Later, by a candlelight that seems almost as golden as the full moon shining through the window, they eat black olives with sheep's cheese and drink the rest of the resinated wine.

"If it were to happen that my life ended now and only this moment were left to me, I would consider it a fulfilled one, I thank you for that Helena."

He raises his glass and gazes at her with his dark eyes at length. In that instant, a dark feeling of dread slithers its way into her heart like a poisonous snake. Immediately her eyes fill with tears. He bends over to her and gently kisses the salty drops away.

"Don't worry, my love, I'm still here," he whispers.

"Please hold me and never let me go."

"Tell me, muse of that man of many resources,
who wandered far and wide, after sacking the holy citadel of Troy. Many the men whose cities he saw, whose ways he learned.

Many the sorrows he suffered at sea, while trying to bring himself and his friends back alive. Yet despite his wishes he failed to save them, because of their own unwisdom, foolishly eating the cattle of Helios, the Sun, so the god denied them their return. Tell us of these things, beginning where you will, Goddess, Daughter of Zeus.

Now, all the others, who had escaped destruction, had reached their homes, and were free of sea and war. He alone, longing for wife and home, Calypso, the Nymph, kept in her echoing cavern, desiring him for a husband. Not even when the changing seasons brought the year the gods had chosen for his return to Ithaca was he free from danger, and among friends. Yet all the gods pitied him, except Poseidon who continued his relentless anger against godlike Odysseus until he reached his own land at last."

They spend the rest of the night, closely intertwined on their island in the middle of the village, with the works of Homer. They submerge themselves into the story of Odysseus, Achilles and Hector, the heroes of Troy.

As morning comes, they slip out of the house as the first cock crows, sniggering like children, who are glad not to have been caught. Helena has left a flower behind as a thank you.

"We'll meet each other again tomorrow under our tree, my love."

The first cocks crow is followed by an answering chorus.

"Unbelievable, that we both saw the same scene." said Sophie, still very moved. "So that is how we know each other. I had the feeling I knew you before, when we were driving back from the airport to Arillas."

"You should have taken my pulse, the first time I saw you. I couldn't understand it at all then ... now I can."

After visiting the old town, that was once their home - a fact that was now clear to the pair of them. - they drove hand in hand through the valley, this was a gesture that in the meantime that had become a habit to them. On the return journey they stopped off at the ice cream parlour. Sophie who had otherwise only ever eaten dairy ice cream, ordered sorbet. Peach and lemon.

"Hmm, that tastes good!" she declared after a while. "You should really break with old traditions once in a while ... otherwise you can really miss out!"

At that moment, the clinic in Muenster seemed to be in an alternative universe and a consultant anaesthetist going by the name of Dr. Sophie Leiter was most probably a woman from Mars.

Apart from that, they didn't speak much. Each were preoccupied with their own thoughts and their feelings for the other, words were not necessary.

"Would you like to go out for dinner this evening?" Rolf asked later.

"Yes, of course ... where shall we go?"

"I think I know of somewhere suitable." he grinned.

Late in the evening, after dinner Rolf took her home. They both got out of the car and embraced their good-byes.

"Thank you for this wonderful day, Rolf, I've a lot to think about right now, sleep well."

She gave him a kiss on the cheek.

"It's me who should be thanking you, I won't forget today, ever.

"Me neither, See you tomorrow, perhaps in the after-noon in Ammos?"

"Of course, I'd love to, sweet dreams."

Once the car had gone, Sophie saw a light still burning in Martha's house.

It is still relatively early, they are probably sitting having dinner right now.

"Do you mind if come in?" asked Sophie.

Martha was busy tidying things into the dishwasher.

She turned around, "What do you look like, Sophie?"

"What do you mean?"

"Somehow you look different to yesterday ... sort of dreamy."

"Well you have probably hit the nail on the head there!" smiled Sophie.

"Come in and sit down, would you like a glass of wine?"

"I've had one already, do you have a beer for me?"

"Beer? I didn't know you drank beer."

"Me neither, until now," laughed Sophie. "But right now, I fancy one."

Martha pulled a bottle out of the fridge and poured a glass. "Talk to me, what is the matter?"

"Unbelieeevable!" she exclaimed once again, after Sophie had recounted it all, "What now?"

"And now? ... Now I believe in reincarnation, that's what. I hardly imagine that the neurons in the Hippocampus of two different people mess about like that at the same time."

"I see Doctor, we are making a scientific conclusion out of this?" smiled Martha. "So, what are you going to do?"

"I love your pragmatism, Martha."

At that moment Kostas came into the kitchen.

"Do you want to leave me sitting out there all on my own?..."

"Oh, I'm so sorry," Sophie got up, "I was just about to leave, it is almost half past ten. I am dog tired. Have a nice evening the pair of you."

Once at the apartment, she did what she had intended doing the whole time. *At home it is only ten o'clock, I'll call Michael. He hasn't done anything to deserve me not calling him.*

She called his number and he answered immediately.

"Hello Michael, I hope I haven't woken you ... but it is only ten o'clock in Germany, are you at home?

"Hi Sophie, good to hear from you ... I thought you had forgotten me already. I didn't go to bed because you said you were going to call. Are you relaxing well? You have been having a hard time lately."

"Yes, I'm doing very well thanks, there is a lot going on here."

"You've met someone, haven't you?"

"Yes ... I have ... but ..."

"It is not that what you think, is what you were going to say next. That's what they all say, isn't it?"

"No, it really isn't that which you think, you can believe me ... please!"

"How is it then?" asked Michael after a short pause. "Sophie, please don't lie to me, I don't deserve that."

"No, you don't either ... and I'm not lying, please Michael ... I would so like to explain it to you."

"You don't have to, I can put two and two together."

"It is really not that simple, I don't understand it myself yet.

"Then I have a suggestion ... would you like to hear it?"

"Of course."

"You have one week's holiday left. During that time, I don't want to have any contact with you, so don't call me ... and when you come back, you are very willing to try and explain everything to me. I think that is the best way."

"If you think so ..." said Sophie sadly.

"Yes, I do think so, Ciao."

Michael hung up abruptly and Sophie had a very disturbed night.

CHAPTER 15

Some of you are still waiting for this mirror. I shall bring those of you who have seen the mirror a step further. I will show you a reflector that will show you every action of your magnificence. You have never seen such a mirror since the first time you came into being on this plane, this mirror however is filled right up with the treasure of wisdom. So be it! (Ramtha)

Friday

In the afternoon they were sitting on a blue bench at Arillas beach, after they had drunk a cappuccino in Ammos. He had laid an arm around her shoulders, a new and yet such an old familiar gesture, but now it provoked her conscience. She twitched slightly. He noticed and withdrew his hand.

"I'm sorry Rolf, it's nothing to do with you. I had a fairly unpleasant conversation with Michael yesterday evening.

"I can understand that, you don't need to explain anything to me."

A white cat came over to them and greeted them, purring.

"Hello, beautiful," she stroked the animal and to Rolf said. "I'm not usually keen on cats, but here I like them."

"That obviously seems to be reciprocated."

The cat sprang onto her lap and settled itself down in such a way, that made it seem as though she was accustomed to it.

"Yesterday evening a white dog came to you and now a white cat has come to me ... strange. I haven't seen any other white cats here at all."

"I find it strange, that she has survived."

"Why?"

"Because she will be immediately spotted by every hunting bird. There are buzzards and falcons here, even eagles fly over from the Albanian mountains."

"Can you remember the grey cat that visited us yesterday evening in Mon Amour?

"Yes of course ... and the white dog."

Yesterday evening they had eaten at *Mon Amour*. Takis Kourkoulos gave them a friendly greeting on arrival.

They had found a place to sit under a cool roof made of vine leaves and colourful ivy. They had blindly followed his recommendation and had ordered lamb and chicken. It tasted good, just as they had anticipated.

A white Labrador had suddenly come in from the street and appeared at his side. Rolf had immediately made friends with the beautiful dog, whose fur felt like silk. The dog stayed for a while, then it moved on to another table, only to reappear soon after. Spiros, the landlord, finally drove it away.

The meal arrived and they drank the strong, red house wine with it, and this had quickly gone to her head. A grey cat sat itself down meowing loudly at her side.

"If you quieten down a little you will get a tasty titbit later on." she had said to the begging cat. They had drunk wine, talked, laughed and been silent. The cat sat silently next to them throughout. Presently, he had forgotten about the cat, but she had kept her promise and not long after the cat disappeared, sated and content.

"I'm going to walk along the beach for a bit," she said and got up. "I'm going to look for wood. I used to do that earlier too. I collected wood. I simply have to do that now."

The cat swapped places from her lap to his. He watched her as she went, searching along the beach. A short time later he followed her at a slight distance on the upper footpath and the cat accompanied him. Then he experienced a completely novelty. He saw Sophie walking down the beach, searching and at the same time had a vision, so it was as if he was watching two films simultaneously.

"Helena, you don't need to carry that. Give me the wood.!"

"I can manage Nikos," she laughs, "You look after your sheep ... look out, the little ones are already running off."

"Kleitos won't let them out of his sight ... look, he is herding them back already. After all, his namesake was one of Alexander the Great's generals."

Then he whistles. The large white sheepdog with the black patches around its eyes came running, after the young animals had been driven back to their mothers.

She puts down the bundle of branches and twigs, kneels down and hugs Kleitos. His long tongue licks her face.

"Hey, you! I've just washed myself at the fountain" she laughs, and he saved the image before him in his mind like a painting.

"Kleitos!"

"Leave him, it's OK"

"You spoil him too much ... he'll go soft and when wolves come in the winter he'll put his tail between his legs."

"You are just being a pessimist, my love. Kleitos is strong, he can take on the whole pack. Can it be, that you're jealous?"

She laughs loudly and he joins in, a sound he loves so much.

"Maybe I am, my love. Did anyone follow you?"

"Lamia wanted to accompany me, but I managed to lose her at the end of the valley. The best wood just happens to be far away from home, she has realised that now. Here, I carved that for you."

She took a small figure out of her pocket.

"A dog!" he calls out in surprise. "You really are an artist, Helena. Thank you, I will always carry it with me. Kleitos, look what Helena has carved out of a piece of olive wood."

He holds the small carving out to the dog who snuffles at it, then ran to Helena and let himself be petted.

"I have you to thank for, that I can do that, Nikos."

"Me? What makes you think that?"

"Collecting wood for my carving was the best explanation that I could think of. That is the only reason why father lets me out of the house for so long. He even encourages me do make more of them. He says that such things are good to sell at the markets in Venice, where rich people spend money on the like."

"One day we will travel there, my love."

"I'm not sure Nikos, how on earth will we manage that? Such a journey costs money and father would never let me leave."

"I'm going to kidnap you!" he jokes good humouredly, takes her in his arms and carries her a stretch up the slope. "You see, that's how easy it is!"

She embraces him and her tears run down his neck. carefully he sets her back down, kisses her and plucks an orange off the tree for her.

"See, it looks like the sun doesn't it?"

Quizzically, she looked up to him and sniffing, wipes the tears away.

"Look very closely, Helena, you are holding a sun in your hands. If you can do that, then you can do any-thing." he laughs.

"You are laughing at me ... "

"No, I would never laugh at you, my beauty. Just think about the hero Odysseus! Everything that he managed to do ... the dangers he survived ... what is a journey to Venice in comparison?"

"I would so love to believe you, Nikos," she whispers, and presses a kiss to his cheek.

"This is what I have found … that one's mine ... and this is for you."

She handed him a small piece of wood in the shape of a spiral.

Swept ashore here together ... like our souls, he thought.

"Thank you, I shall keep it and think of you when I look at it."

But he knew that he didn't need a piece of wood to be able to do that.

"This evening I am going to take you to Afionas for dinner. Would you like to go to Anemos?"

"Of course, I've been there already, I drank an Ouzo there. It is a lovely place, I'll look forward to it!"

"By the way, I have to go into town again tomorrow. Mr. Takahashi wants to meet up with me again. Angeliki will be there too. He insists on inviting us to eat with him and his wife, so we probably won't be able to see each other tomorrow, Sophie."

"Oh, I am pleased for you. It sounds as though he is quite serious about it all, doesn't it? I'm going to go for a ride on the motor scooter tomorrow, otherwise it will have been a waste renting it, if I let you ferry me about all the time. And the rest of the day I shall spend in my hammock with the Durrell book."

CHAPTER 16

Now there are very, very few soul mates who have actually encountered each other physically. They are rare, rare, rare! If they meet before they have mastered their barriers, the matrimony is explosive because each one will be confronted with their complete pettiness all at once. It is as though one would be wrestling with one's self. And how often have you made yourself miserable and unhappy? Well, multiply that number by itself. (Ramtha)

Sunday

"So, how was your day?" asked Rolf, after he had picked Sophie up from her apartment. She had been sitting on the steps waiting for him expectantly.
"Very relaxing, I did what I planned to do, and I have finished reading the book. It was really enjoyable, not just his prose but also his lively descriptions about how life was previously.
"In the evening I had dinner in Gravia. The view from there is fantastic ... my God, I have used that word so much ... but it is true. The two brothers Kostas and Yiannis are very friendly. I can't remember how many times Kostas thanked me. Have you ever experienced a landlord in Germany who thanked you for being permitted to bring you something? If I owned a restaurant, I would send my apprentices to Gravia for training, so they can learn what real customer service is. The

calamari was excellent. Later, I went to a mantra concert in the wonderful seminar room above Gravia with Martha. Even bought the CD from Petra. How was your day? You probably did a lot more than me."

"Angeliki would now say 'Meeega successful'" he smiled, "but it was, really. Mr. Takahashi is a very decisive person. We met in the gallery and he explained his plans to us there. He is going to publish a long article in three newspapers and then exhibit my photographs in the *National Art Center* in Tokyo, imagine, he has also bought the series 'People in Corfu.' You are my lucky charm, Sophie!"

"Luck is for dummies, that's what I've heard," retorted Sophie with a smile, "No, you have worked hard and earned your success and it was absolutely right that you followed your instinct."

"Over dinner, we discussed that as early as in September, Angeliki will be flying to Tokyo. You will never guess where we went."

"I wonder where!" laughed Sophie.

"You're right."

"And? How was the Japanese verdict?"

"Japanese," grinned Rolf. "Mr. Takahashi said it was tasty, but we definitely have to try the sushi in his country as well."

"Very diplomatic." smiled Sophie.

"I see you are wearing your trainers, do you fancy going for a hike?"

"A hike? Yes, OK, where are we going to go?"

"To Afionas and Anemos. Then, if we manage, I'll show you the famous double bay and the grotto."

"Come on then, let's go!"

Rolf parked his Jeep in the Graziella restaurant car park, and they set off from there.

A picturesque path lead from there to Afionas which was about four hundred metres higher up. Sophie stopped frequently to take photos with her phone.

"There's something the matter with you, Sophie, do you want to tell me what's up?" said Rolf after a while.

"I can't hide anything from you, can I? Well you're right. A little drop of woe has fallen into my colourful Greek cocktail."

"So how did that happen?"

"You know, the chat with Michael."

"And?"

"I told that I had met you ... I wanted to be honest. I haven't called him as often as I usually do ... we usually call each other every evening ... but I didn't get any further than that, because he ... well took it like men often do ... anyway, he said he thought it may be better if we didn't contact each other until the end of my holiday, then he hung up."

"And how do you feel about it?"

"At first I was upset ... but I can understand him too. When I get home I'm sure I will have the opportunity to explain everything to him ... and if he really loves me, he'll cope with it. Perhaps it'll prove to be a good test for our relationship."

They didn't speak much for the rest of the walk.

Afionas has a spectacular location on a peninsular above *St George's beach*. It is a scenic little village with houses in the typical Greek style, however during the holiday season it is firmly in the hands of the tourists. If you like traffic jams, it is the place to be in August and September. Although several years ago a large car park was built below the village, plenty of rental cars squeeze themselves through, up to the little church, this is a particular cause of outrage amongst the bus drivers for whom turning under such circumstance proves exceedingly difficult. Aside of that the village has been able to maintain its unique Greek charm.

The best way to discover the pretty village is to take a walk around. You can tell that with time, artists have settled here. Little stone cottages with lush flower gardens bewitch the blue of the sea with thousands of colourful highlights, sleepy alleyways lend thought to heavily packed donkeys, which delivered the villagers with goods in days gone by. The path through the village ends at a square with three benches. From there one has a panoramic view of the Ionian Sea. First in view is the island of *Gravia* in the bay of *Arillas*. On the hill between *Arillas* and *St. Stefanos* is a restaurant with the same name which, run with friendliness and good spirits by the two brothers Kostas and Yiannis Mouzakitis. It is well worth a visit, not only for the two of them, but also for the grandiose view. There is fresh fish of course, that their father, Christos, had caught in the morning. Higher up the *Akrotiri* is most welcoming, with its tasteful furnishings. At sundown the view from the flat roof of the Lounge café is a must. The culinary delights at the Akrotiri should also not be missed.

When she arrived in Afionas and went passed the *Three Brothers*, Sophie told herself that she most certainly would visit the little shop near the church.

"I saw it whilst I was sitting up there on a bench, but it was closed at the time ... My God, is that only a few days ago? I feels like ages ago."

"Somehow it is though." said Rolf.

The shop *'Olives and More'* is run by a German couple who sell the best olive oil and a selection of special souvenirs.

"Oh, look at that sign, there's a piece of land up for sale, I'd like to have a look."

"You'd like to buy a piece of land?"

"No, not me, but my parents dream of spending their retirement years somewhere in the south and when I spoke to them yesterday and was in raptures about Corfu, my father asked me about the price of land here."

They followed the little path to the point where a mighty fig tree stood. from here they had an uninterrupted view of the bay of *Arillas*.

"It is a beautiful view," he said, "but in the height of the season thousands of tourist tramp about up here. Furthermore, it is miles from the sea, you would definitely need a car."

Later when she came out of the little shop, she saw him leaning against an old iron fence, looking lost. She approached him and gave him a hug. On so doing, her gaze fell on a sweet little white cottage, with blue shutters and geraniums, that she hadn't noticed the last time they came here. Her breathing came heavy and tears sprang into her eyes, her heart felt as though it would burst out of her chest, like it did a few days ago in *Paleo Perithia*.

"I have to go in there on my own," she said, breathing hard and pointed to the little alleyway, which lead into the old part of the village.

Rolf felt immediately that this was a very special moment for Sophie.

He watched her, as she ran towards the house. In front of the door she stood still and held her hands before her eyes.

"Yaya, dearest Yaya!" She runs to her Grandmother and falls into her arms. The old woman laughs and hugs Helena close. This is her favourite grandchild, a fact she will of course admit to no-one.

"How lovely it is to see you, little Helena," exclaims Agada, not wanting to let go. "How tall you have become ... and so pretty!"

She strokes her youngest granddaughter's black hair which she is wearing down that day. "How long has it been since we last saw each other, my child?"

"Far too long Yaya ... far too long!"

"Even your last letter was over two moons ago. I am always so happy, when you write to me ... that way I can still be a part of your life. If I had known you were coming I would have cooked your favourite meal, come into the house and tell me all your news. There is something to tell, I can see it in your face."

She immediately starts to cry. "He wants to leave, Yaya...."

"Who wants to leave, tell me child?"

"Nikos", she sobs loudly.

"Nikos? Why?"

"Spiros has asked father for my hand for him."

"He did that for you two? But it is obvious how that will end. You know your father, I know your father, we all know him. He will never agree to a marriage with anyone who doesn't come from a wealthy house. What on earth was Spiros thinking about. Hasn't you father already chosen a husband for you? Your mother wrote to me and told me."

"Yes, he has, Yaya. I've been introduced to him already. The family comes from Constantinople and belongs to the nobility. They are very, very wealthy. He is called Alexios, is fat and has a hare lip." first she giggles, then the tears start flowing again.

"I visited the holy Spiridon every day and have begged him to help me. I don't know how many candles I have lit to him."

"Did Spiros know about your father's plans?"

"Yes, I told him all about it, but he still wanted to try Yaya." She sobs even louder.

"Now Nikos is in danger, and Spiros too, do you realise that? Your father will not rest until both of them have left your village ... no, the whole area."

"That's why Nikos wants to leave and ..."

"And what, child?"

"He wants to go to Venice, because he thinks he can become a rich man there. Then he wants to come back and marry me. He has gone to Kassiopi to find work of passage on a ship."

"Did he say that? It is dangerous, the sea is dangerous! There are pirates!"

"He is not scared of any of that, Yaya."

"Your father will find you anywhere. You know what possibilities he possesses."

"Then I shall join an abbey, I shall never marry another, no matter how rich he is!"

When Sophie returned, she was in tears and Rolf took her spontaneously into his arms. They stood like that for a long time, as if they were marooned on some lonely island. They were oblivious to the many tourists milling around.

Stuttering and broken up by the many sobs, Sophie recounted her story and Rolf listened intently without interrupting her once.

Once she had regained her composure a little, Rolf said to Sophie:

"Come on, let's go and have something to eat in Anemos, it'll do us the world of good."

"Yes, you're right, let's do that."

Whilst they ate grilled calamari and sardines, they kept getting back on to the subject of their common past so long ago.

"What else are we going to see?" queried Sophie, "I've become really quite curious. Whether we know each other from further lives? What do you think?"

"I have no idea, but it is possible. If you ask me, it is enough to cope with knowing you out of one past life at the moment."

"If I were to tell someone in the clinic about all this, they would consider me mad and check me into the psychiatric ward!" she said, smiling.

"Then don't spread it around! Although, when I look at the world at the moment, there seem to be far less insane people in the Psychiatric department, than outside of it! Do you still fancy going to the double bay?"

"You know what, I think I have had enough walking for one day, we still have to walk all the way back. I would like to stay here for a while."

"Then that is what we'll do. It is probably very crowded down there already, almost everyone walks down to it. You have to come early in the morning, then it is even quiet enough to swim."

"Let's go down there in a day or two, the weather is supposed to stay fine, at least according to my App."

"Then I'll order us another coffee."

"This evening Kostas and Martha want to take me to Brouklis to eat, why don't you come with us?"

"I'm afraid I can't this evening, I have a Yoga class with Torsten in the Ouranos Club, but perhaps we could see each other later in Akrotiri, it is a little further away from Gravia, up the hill."

"Yes, I saw that already, when I was with the beekeeper. Martha said it was an absolute must to buy honey there. I must have sat on the swinging chair for at least an hour. Wonderful."

It was late in the afternoon when the pair of them set off to return to Arillas.

CHAPTER 17

Don't do anything that doesn't fill you with joy. If you do it anyway, it means that you don't love yourself. Be fair to yourself. Do that which brings you joy, despite everyone else. Do it for the sake of the God inside you. Reach for it! (Ramtha)

"It's a good job I reserved," commented Martha, after they had taken their places at the last free table in *Brouklis*. "It is always full in here and you'll find out why in a minute."

"It is very romantic under the roof of vines," said Sophie having a look around, "It's a shame that the grapes aren't ripe yet though."

A waiter brought them the menu.

Sophie ordered deep fried courgette balls, roasted sardines and a Greek salad.

"Shall we have a beer with the meal?" asked Kostas, and when the two women nodded, he also ordered lentil soup and fried Aubergine with chicken.

"We can share it can't we, Agape Mou"?

"What exactly does 'Agape Mou' mean?" asked Sophie.

"My love," or 'my darling'" answered Kostas.

"Well, now I have something that you can't possibly know!" said Martha, after the waiter had brought their beer.

"Now I'm curious!" smirked Sophie.

"Where does the German word 'Klimaanlage' come from?"

Sophie pondered over it.

"I have no idea, tell me."

"You are sitting underneath it!" laughed her friend. "Klimateria is the Greek expression for vine foliage. In the summer it gives us shade and in the winter when the leaves have been lost, it lets the warming sun through."

"That is quite interesting .... and logical. I did think that it had roots in the Greek language though. - Oh look, here comes your soup!"

After the meal, Sophie said: "I now realize why the taverns are so full, although they are right at the road-side and you can't see the sea from here."

"Some time ago you could though," explained Kostas, "I can still remember the time when you could see all the way over to the island of Gravia. In those days the tavern was still called Gravia."

"Good evening Dimitris!" Kostas greeted the man who had come to their table. "May I introduce our guest Sophie to you? She is one of Martha's former colleagues ... and this is Dimitris, the owner of this wonderful restaurant!"

Dimitris shook everyone by the hand and sat himself down at the table.

"I have just explained to Sophie how it used to look here, when your father still ran the place and that you could see the sea from here."

"That is right." said Dimitris, turning to Sophie, "There were hardly any houses, Arillas was a sleepy little nest near the sea. But we were already the first to be who were using climate neutral and purely organic means of transport."

"I beg your pardon?" asked Sophie, amazed.

"Yes, I was about five years old, but I can remember it quite well. We used to have a summer house where we lived ... maybe four hundred metres to the west. A path lead from here over to it. If I had to go home, my father would sit me on a donkey, give it a whack on its hindquarters and ten minutes later I was home!"

"Delightful!" laughed Sophie.

"Well, I'd better get back to work," said Dimitri, excusing himself. "I hope you enjoy the rest of your evening and for you Sophie, a relaxing holiday."

"Are we going to go to Akrotiri? Rolf wants to go there after his Yoga class too.

"Yes, we are," replied Martha, winking. "As long as we don't disturb the pair of you."

"Funny." said Sophie. "You just can't leave it be, can you?"

"Oh, come on!"

When they arrived at Akrotiri, Rolf was already there. He was sitting a table on the veranda in front of the entrance with a glass of beer and recognised Kostas' car immediately.

"Good to see you. I wouldn't have been able to keep your seats for much longer, you can see how busy it is."

He hugged the ladies and clapped a greeting on Kostas shoulder.

"Where have all the people come from?" enquired Sophie and looked all around. "It is nice here."

She seated herself next to Rolf and gave him a kiss on the cheek.

"From Ouranos, Zorbas or Mythos. Below us here is even a small seminar room and sometimes in the morning they do Tai Chi or the sun greeting on the roof." explained Martha. "An authentic location for a seminar ... next to Gravia and Ammos."

The young owner came over to their table to take their orders.

"Hello Kostas," he said, after he had greeted them all, "Good to see you here again, too."

"Well, Nikos, you know how it is, during the season there is always plenty to do, but then, you are aware about that ... and since Maria arrived we don't go out much anymore. We wanted to show our friend the Akrotiri ... Rolf is the regular here."

"He is called Nikos!" whispered Sophie to Rolf, smiling, "Like you did previously."

"That is not difficult," he whispered back. "Sometimes I get the impression that there are only four names used on this island. Nikos, Spiros, Vassilis and Kostas."

"Are you going to have an Aperol, Sophie?" asked Martha.

"Sure, I don't need to drive back. I'll be able to manage that distance even after two glasses."

"And if it should be more, I'll drive you!" grinned Rolf.

"That might just happen!" laughed Sophie.

"Hey what do you take me for! Martha, help me won't you?"

"I'm keeping well out of this, If I say anything about that," said Martha dryly, "I'll be in trouble with Sophie."

"You are absolutely right, my dear!"

They all laughed.

"It is really very enjoyable here, I even like the music," said Sophie, after the drinks had arrived. The men kept to their beer.

"The Akrotiri has a nice story," said Kostas. "The grandfather of the Mouzakitis, that's the brothers in the Gravia, is supposed to have sold this piece of land to grandfather Gourdelis for a couple of Drachma. As you have seen, up here it is fairly rocky and sometimes it can be very stormy here in the winter, neither tree nor vine grows here. So, it wasn't worth much. Who would have thought back then that one day tourists would come? Nikos opened the Akrotiri a few years ago. These days you could earn a pretty penny for all of this."

"That is similar to how it was on Sylt earlier," commented Sophie. "These days the jet set all gather there and the land costs millions. Can you remember how much fun we had that time, when we ... with....," Sophie paused.

Kostas laughed, "Sophie, I know all about Dr. Hansen. We know about each other's past, isn't that right, Agape Mou?"

"Yes, my love, and you know how happy I am, that we met here. It was the most beautiful holiday I have ever had, it couldn't have been better."

"For me neither."

"How was your Yoga, Rolf?" asked Sophie.

"Very good, as always, Torsten is very good."

"Were you in his practice in Afionas?" asked Martha

"No, here in Ouranos."

"I think that I'm going to try it one day ... and it would do you some good too, my dear. That would be fun, to do it together."

"Please, spare me!" laughed Kostas, "If I do it all, I'd do it here at Claudia's."

Martha nudged him jovially in his side. "No chance of that, my dear!"

The rest of the evening was spent with the telling of stories and laughing. At some point Sophie checked her watch.

"Oh my God, it is already one o'clock! I must get off to bed! What about the rest of you?"

"I reckon, we're going too," said Martha, "Although Maria is sleeping at her grandparents, but it's time for me to go too. What have you got planned for tomorrow?"

"I'm leaving that to Rolf!" grinned Sophie, "He is the tour operator!"

Rolf got up.

"May I cordially invite you? Tomorrow will be full of tourism, Sophie, I'm going to show you Paleokastritsa and if there is enough time, Pelekas with the 'Kaiser's Throne.'"

"Super! I can't wait!"

"That will be a good day" remarked Martha, "Shall we take you with us now, or do you want to walk?"

"I'll come with you."

"And we'll see each other tomorrow, Sophie, shall we say nine o'clock?"

"Would ten o'clock be OK too?"

"Of course, ten is OK," laughed Rolf and hugged Sophie goodbye.

In the car, Sophie said: "Thank you so much for this wonderful evening, Martha, I understand more from day to day, just how much you like living here!"

CHAPTER 18

Now you are beginning to achieve wisdom, and a knowledge and a fearlessness, that you never possessed before. And although your soul mate is not quite sure about what is happening in their lives, no matter what it is, it is wonderful. Your soul mates will react completely instinctively to your actions and he will begin to possess a hiding place with supplies. It will be completely natural for him and whilst he carries out his actions he gives you the support you need to feel good doing what you are doing. That way you grow together. Do you understand? Whatever you do, you do for each other, for the completeness of yourself. (Ramtha)

Monday

The next morning, Sophie was waiting on the street punctually at ten o'clock. She was wearing a red dress and she had put her hair up, over her shoulder she had slung the little green rucksack that she had bought in Arillas, in her hand she held a sun hat.

As Rolf drove around the corner and saw her standing there, he stopped the car for a moment.

Sophie waved.

"Good morning!" she said happily, "Why have you stopped?"

"I wanted to enjoy the charming view for a moment. Such a shame that I haven't brought my camera with me!" he smiled.

"Funny guy!" said Sophie and gave him a kiss on the cheek.

"No, I'm not joking at all, you look fantastic. Red really is your colour."

"Thank you! And I like it when you wear white, as you are doing now."

"Yeah, sure, because it reminds you of the clinic," he said ironically.

"You funny guy, keep it up!"

"My pleasure, it is one of my favourite past times."

"Oh my God, what have I done to deserve this?"

"That question you will have to answer for yourself ... you'll like the drive to Paleokastritsa, it is one of the most beautiful on the whole of Corfu, you'll see."

On the way he had to stop many times, so that Sophie could get out of the car to take photos.

Paleokastritsa is most probably the most popular holiday resort on the west coast. Its name means *Old Castle Square* and bears reference to the castle that can be seen from there, the *Angelokastro*. The region consists of two peninsulas and five bays that are among the most beautiful on the island. There is no town centre in the middle though. Hotels, houses and taverns are scattered over the landscape and are often hidden amongst olive trees and cypresses. Two other villages, *Doukades* and *Gardelades*, also belong to the community.

The location at the foot of steep hills is spectacular. Lush green woodlands with cypress and olive trees alongside the Ionian Sea with its deep blue and turquoise waters dominate the impressive landscape.

The actual village of *Paleokastritsa*, at the end of the street which snakes its way down to the sea, is quite diminutive. The hotels and other accommodation hardly disturb the charming sight of the surroundings at all.

The sandy beaches belonging to the little bays boast crystal clear water. You can take boats to countless other incredible beaches or swim to well situated caves and cliffs.

The main attraction is the *Panagia Theotokos* abbey, which is located high up on a peninsula with sheer descending cliffs. It was founded in the thirteenth century and was extended to its momentary form which reflects the architecture of the Kykladen, of the eighteenth and nineteenth centuries. The church is consecrated to Mary, Mother of God, has a painted ceiling and icons in the Ionic style of the eighteenth century and is surrounded by a colourful flower garden, a beautiful cell wing and leafy walkways. The cloistered court with the free-standing Venetian bell tower, the fountain and an old oil and grape press on the lower storey are also well worth seeing. Interesting Icons and works of art are exhibited in a small museum. The monastery is a magnificent motive for photographs and offers lovely views all around. The painted ceiling of the single-nave church portrays the Father, Son and - in the form of a dove - the Holy Spirit. The most valuable Icon found in the church is at the front on the left-hand side wall. The artwork, dating back to the year 1653, measures a mere forty-three times thirty-three centimetres, it depicts three Church Fathers in their magnificent robes. Beneath it there is a dramatic scene represented, one which did actually occur in the town of Kerkyra. As a firework exploded, a child's nurse who was standing nearby with her charge in her arms, was killed. Miraculously, the child remained un-scathed. The nanny is clearly visible on the right-hand side of the picture: With blood pouring out of her left flank, she sinks to the ground, still cradling the child. The parents donated the Icon in thanks to the saints for this miracle.

"What a sensational garden, Rolf, please come over here and have a look at the view."

"Yes, the monasteries are invariably built in incredible surroundings, I've heard that special powers are present there."

"So how did the find out about it?" laughed Sophie, "With a divination rod?"

"Why not?"

"Do you believe in such things?"

"Well, I've not tried it myself, but ..."

"You've read about it ... is that it?"

They both had to laugh.

In the church they had sat silently, hand in hand and regarded the wonderful wall paintings. On leaving the monastery, he threw a coin into the fountain.

"You are not allowed to say what you have wished for," he explained, on noticing her querying look.

"Then I shall throw one in too."

They found a free table at a nearby café.

"Look, can you see the rocks in the sea? According to Homer it is supposed to be the petrified ship, the one that Poseidon transformed into stone as it was about to sail Odysseus back to his home in Ithaca. He is supposed to have landed, shipwrecked, in the small heart-shaped cove, that we saw before. At that moment the princess Nausikaa and her companions were playing there. An ancient love story began and also tragically ended here."

"Did you also read Homer in *this* life as well?"

"I didn't have much choice, I took Greek at school and believe me it was absolute torture ... but exciting in the end."

"Well I don't think the rocks look anything like a ship, more like a bat, lying down."

"Mm, I can see an otter, which is lying in the water with a shell in its paws."

And so it carried on for a while, back and forth, between her bat and his otter. They couldn't reach an agreement on it.

Sophie paid for the drinks and afterwards the drove down the winding road to *Lakones,* a mountain village.

"It is very narrow here, it's a good job that there is a traffic light." said Sophie.

"It didn't used to be here. When I came here years ago with my parents we drove through this village too. At the time it was the run up to the elections and on the small square that we are coming up to, the communist party were having an event, with flags, music and an unbelievable number of people.

"Of all the parties, we meet the communists, his father had said back then. In any case, we couldn't travel any further. A man asked us to get out of the car because the whole street was blocked. He could speak German quite well. We then did so and later we were invited to the ensuing festivities. In those days there was only a small tavern there. My mother said to my father: *Seeing as though we are here, Frank, we should accept their invitation, we wanted to get to know the real Greek way of life after all. It's here.* I think it was way past midnight when we carried on our journey. That is to say, my mother carried it on, because my old man was too drunk!" Rolf laughed. "I still laugh about it today. My father partied with the communists! At the time he admired Franz Josef Strauss. You wouldn't believe how often we have teased him about it since then!"

"Something like that is never forgotten!" grinned Sophie.

At the restaurant, *Golden Fox*, they took a short break. On the narrow balcony, on which he had often sat to eat, Sophie was as enraptured, as many were before her, on seeing the view from there for the first time. She could hardly get over her amazement. Her eyes wandered over the three heart shaped coves to the wooded hills, which carried on out into the plains.

"So, Odysseus got stranded down there?"

"According to legend, yes." said Rolf.

They ordered coffee and cake and enjoyed the wonderful view.

"I think, it is going to start again with me" said Rolf, quietly.

"What's going to start?"

"I can see pictures."

"Really? And you can talk at the same time?"

"I think so."

The taproom is full to bursting with beer swilling men. A smoggy haze of sweat, stale beer, sour wine and roasted fish drifts through the tavern. It was on the road between Perithia and Kassiopi. They wouldn't have been able to meet up unnoticed in either of those two places. Even so, Helena's father's spies could almost certainly be everywhere.

"Thank you for doing that for me ... for us, Spiros ... even though it hasn't quite worked out, how I hoped it would ... in my wildest dreams I mean ... but in cold light of day, it was predestined for disaster."

"I did it gladly for you Nikos, even though I didn't set my hopes too high. I'm just glad that he didn't set the dogs on me."

Spiros smiles, wryly.

"I think that Socrates saying applies to her father fairly well ... *Are you not ashamed about caring so much for money and the making of it; when you neither think nor care about insight and truth and the wellbeing of your soul.*"

"He wouldn't really understand your Socrates."

"I am so glad that Helena doesn't take after her father in the slightest ... even though she loves him so much."

"It's clear that he would never agree to your marriage under these circumstances."

"Unless ..." Nikos cupped his head in his hands, "I become wealthy."

"How on earth will you manage that ... up here in the mountains?"

"In Venice, my friend, in Venice. I will go to Venice. There are many possibilities there ... I have heard about it. I will take on any work that gets paid. Perhaps I'll get lucky."

"You are insane, my friend. How will you get there? Passage is expensive and stowaways get thrown overboard."

"I'll think of something."

"And what are you going to tell your parents? You know that your mother will be troubled. What your father will say doesn't bear thinking about."

"I'll explain it to them, I'll think of something."

"And who will shepherd the sheep? You know that I have enough to do with my carpentry."

"Yes, my friend, I know that. I am going to talk with Georgios' father, he will be fourteen soon and could do it."

The peace and quiet was interrupted by a group of travellers. They took photographs and were conversing loudly.

Rolf opened his eyes.

"It's unbelievable how clearly you saw it all, whilst being here."

"I have the impression that the pictures get clearer the more often they come. It really is as though I were watching a film at the cinema. In colour and with sound."

"Yes, that is how I feel it too, especially after we were in Perithia."

"Let's get going again, otherwise we will have the bus in front of us the whole way. Up here, overtaking is almost impossible."

"And where are we going to now? My stomach has just started grumbling, despite the cake."

"If you can wait just a little longer, we could have something to eat at the beach in Pelekas or higher up in the restaurant at Kaiser's Throne."

"I'm going to leave it entirely up to you, up until now everything's been fine."

Once they had got into the car, Rolf's mobile rang.

"Hmm, an unknown number. I don't usually answer them. I'll make an exception this time though, it could be Mr. Takahashi. Is that alright?"

"Of course."

"Rolf accepted the call.

"Who is it? ... Herbert? Herbert who? Whaaat, you? Where on earth did you get my number? How are you? I've not heard anything from you in ages ... Where are you tomorrow? ... In Corfu? ... you've got married? ... Glad to, one moment, I'll ring you back in a tic."

Rolf was still holding the mobile phone in his hand.

"That was an old school friend of mine, Herbert. My mother gave him my number, he's only got the German one, this here is my Greek phone.

"Wonders will never cease! He has got married and arrives tomorrow on the AIDA in Corfu. He always thought he would never find a soul mate. Typical bachelor guy. They want to meet me in town tomorrow ..."

"That's terrific, you do that ... then I'll have a girls' day out with Martha, we'd been planning to, anyway."

"I'll ring him back right away. I can't wait to meet his wife."

CHAPTER 19

The man, who does not know how to cry, who lives with hemmed in emotions, who is furious, who is hurt and doesn't know how to free his feelings - if he can understand this science then he can bring himself closer to his other self, the feminine side of his being and he can enter her soul and take everything with him, that he carries within himself. He can enter her spirit and her soul and can begin to cry like a child and perhaps shed a thousand tears. Those tears will compensate for seven and a half million years of suppressed fear, fury, hurt and confusion, that were not allowed to be expressed. (Ramtha)

The west coast has a multitude of beautiful beaches. Of them all, the beach at *Pelekas* is a gem. It may be reached via a small road which turns off from the incoming road to the town, about level with a wall covered in graffiti. Wide and with the finest sand, it spans the entire length of the bay. Next to taverns and a mini supermarket, the Hotel *Pelekas Beach* is situated at the southernmost end of the beach.

They had ordered their meal and were looking at the beach, which was quite crowded.

"The first time I came here there were only a couple of bamboo huts over there at the end. It was a paradise for hippies, simply wonderful. It almost breaks my heart to look over to the cliffs and see the giant hotels."

A gentle sea breeze played with the fronds of her hair and she combed a lock back from her forehead and commented: "That is the price of tourism and if you don't know it any other way ... well I think it is lovely here."

"It is too, that is the reason why I wanted to show it to you."

They ate Greek salad with an extra portion of Feta and shared the grilled calamari, accompanied by a light white wine.

"I think this cuttlefish is becoming my favourite meal here," said Sophie, "Sushi I can get in Muenster too."

"I like it a lot too, particularly because it is prepared differently in the various places."

"Do you often come here?"

"No, only for the festival. Then lots of musicians meet up and there is good live music. I always show my visitors Pelekas of course, most of all for the Kaiser's Throne with the magnificent view. It was built by Wilhelm II. It is said that he went over there to meditate. We'll drive up there after the meal, unless you fancy having a swim beforehand."

"I'd love to, but I haven't got my bathing things with me."

"Then let's go there after the meal, the village of Pelekas will appeal to you."

"An oakwood!" Sophie cried out in surprise on arriving at the Kaiser's Throne.

Rolf laughed. "

"Of course, a German Emperor would have an oak-wood planted! Come on, just these stairs and then we're there."

He took Sophie by the hand.

"Wow! That is really sensational," Sophie called out a moment later. "You can almost see the whole island!"

"Yes, it's really fantastic!"

"Do you think that we had been here before? I mean on this mountain, the Throne wasn't here then."

"I don't think so, at least I don't have the feeling that we did."

"I'd like to sit here for a while," said Sophie, "Even if people keep on coming up."

"Then we shall do so."

During the whole hour they spent at the lookout point, they heard at least five different languages. It became crowded when a touring coach emptied its freight at the car park, but the tourists didn't stay long.

"That's another programme point ticked off," said Rolf wryly, once the bus had set back off on its way.

"There wasn't a single Japanese person amongst them."

"Well, if you only have a few days holiday a year, you are pushed for time."

The both laughed and suddenly kissed each other for the very first time. At first, like children trying an unknown fruit, then quickly becoming adult.

"We shouldn't do that," panted Sophie, breathing heavily.

"Why not? Didn't you like it?"

"As if you didn't notice!" smiled Sophie, "You know exactly what I mean."

"Michael."

"Yes, Michael, I wouldn't like it either, the other way around."

"I can understand that, but it was just so spontaneous ... it felt right to me."

"It did for me too, Rolf, but it really must stop there."

"You have a bad conscience, haven't you?"

"Yes of course I have, it is against my moral principles."

"But a bad conscience has nothing to do with morals.

"With what then, Mr. Know-it-all?"

"It is the fear of not belonging anymore."

"That's right, it is that. My grandmother used to say: *a good conscience is a comfortable pillow.*"

"Then she must have known how it feels to have a bad conscience. In any case, I am now going to keep a special and unique memory of the Kaiser's Throne in my heart and can appreciate Nikos feelings for Helena ... Oh, wait a moment, then it isn't a unique memory at all."

She bent towards him and kissed him. This time even more passionately.

"So, that one was from Helena for Nikos, the first one was for Rolf ... and now that's that!"

He grinned. "Wow, this Helena is really crafty, maybe we'll discover even more common lives."

"Stop it!" Smiling, she nudged him in the ribs. "Come on let's go, I have had enough of this Throne."

They drove through silent olive groves and little villages in the Jeep and as they drove down one road which offered a panoramic view of both sides of the island, she kept repeating how beautiful she found it all.

"What do think of having dinner in Anemos this evening?" asked Rolf as they drove through the village of Agros.

"Can you read my mind? I was just thinking exactly the same just now. The Anemos has a special meaning to me, because that is where I had my first vision. I just didn't want to mention it, because I didn't want you to consider me greedy"

"No, I can't read thoughts and I don't want to be able to either."

At dinner they talked about the day out, however, they avoided what had happened at the Kaiser's Throne.

At the neighbouring table there was a family with three children, who were all preoccupied with their mobile phones.

"Very practical for the parents," said Rolf, "That way the parents have a little peace."

"Yes, and we have no lack of patients because in thirty years' time they all present with damaged stature, heart and circulatory diseases and adiposity. They hardly move themselves anymore."

"And have no idea anymore, of their whereabouts."

"Do you have any siblings?" asked Sophie.

"Yes, an older sister, who I have much to thank for. She gave me some considerable support when I gave up my architecture career. And you?"

"I had a younger brother ..."

"Had?"

"Yes, unfortunately he died when he was three years old. I was nine at the time."

"What did he die of?"

"Of Hib, that caused a severe bacterial meningitis, he must have got infected with it somewhere, probably at nursery school.

"Is that the reason you became a doctor?"

"I have thought that over for while too, perhaps, yes. But let's talk about something else, it's such a lovely day."

At that moment the landlord approached the table.

"Well you too, what can I offer you now? Today we have a very delicious apple pie."

"Shall we share a piece?" asked Rolf, "I'll burst otherwise."

"Yes let's ... it doesn't matter now anyway, so please bring us one piece of apple pie with two forks and an espresso for me. For you too, Rolf?"

"Yes, I'll take one too, sleep is overrated anyway!" he grinned.

"I have to vehemently disagree with you there, my dear."

"Was a joke, I actually sleep quite a lot. I have almost accustomed myself to nature's rhythm."

"So, you are an early riser too?"

"Very early in fact, I have the best ideas then and at midday I often have a siesta at the beach ... so I must be bursting with health."

"Don't you then? I haven't got my doctor's bag with me," laughed Sophie. "but you aren't insured anyway."

"I pay cash, that is quite popular here."

"And then you will inform on me to the tax office, won't you? Can I ask you something else?"

"You may ask anything."

"Have you been married before? Apologies for my curiosity!"

"A question I would rather not answer ..."

"Why not?"

"If I answer with yes, it means: Aha, not capable of relationships, if it is negated: Aha, scared of attachment. But I'll gladly give you an answer ... yes I was once married ... Mia was my childhood romance.

"We had known each other since primary school and shortly before the final school exams we became a couple. We went to Corfu on our honeymoon, can you remember? Renault 4 with dashboard gears? That is now twenty years ago. I think she loved this island more than me, if there are superlatives of love at all. Whilst we were on our honeymoon she became pregnant ..."

"You have a child? How lovely!..."

"Wait a moment, let me finish ... when she was seven months pregnant she was run over ... the driver had over two permille, was eighteen and only had a driving licence for a week, Mia and the baby were killed instantly ... it was terrible ... it would have been a boy and we wanted to call him Alexander."

"Oh my God, how tragic ... I'm so sorry!"

"It took me three years to get over it and at least one of those years in therapy. It was five years before I felt capable to return here. I didn't actually want to come back to Corfu, but it turned out to be exactly the right decision. It was here that I was able to deal with the situation completely, though it took a further two years before I could start a relationship with another woman. If it is true, that you have only one real love in life, then it was Mia."

Sophie stood up and embraced him.

"Thank you for sharing that with me ... and how is it for you now, when you are showing me all of these places?"

"That is completely different, and I can enjoy it a lot ... I hope that you have noticed that. And how about you? Have you been married?"

"Yes, once. I hate to talk about it because it sounds like such a terrible cliché.

"Now I'm curious."

"Oh, well, ... young junior doctor starts her first job and fall in love with the handsome consultant, who to start with looks after her lovingly ... the rest you can imagine for yourself."

"He looked after others too?"

"Yes, and me the idiot was the last to notice. Perhaps love really does make you blind."

"On that note I'm going to order us an Ouzo, Is that alright with you?"

"You can say that again!"

It turned into two.

Shortly afterwards they left Anemos, laughing.

The pie was really delicious," said Sophie, "Although I am now full to bursting."

"Shall we drive to Akrotiri to have a nightcap?"

Sophie thought for a moment.

"I'd rather not. I've had enough for today, I'm dead tired as well. The alcohol is beginning to work, I'd rather just fall into bed."

"Shall I come with you? I could sing you a lullaby."

"Funny guy!" she laughed, "Just bring me home and be quiet!"

CHAPTER 20

Do you know why you are so unhappy? Be-cause you are afraid of change; You are scared of get-ting involved in something unfamiliar. That is why you are bored, pathetic, miserable, suicidal creatures! That summarizes it, doesn't it?

Think about it for a moment. Are you stuck with the same lover? Do you still live in the same desolate place? Are you still working in the same monotonous job? Yet you still don't change anything, because you are scared. But did you know that in the future 'now', there is nothing to fear? Nothing! (Ramtha)

Tuesday

"I am so glad that we finally have a whole day to ourselves!" said Martha as they left the driveway in her car.

"Yes, it's perfect, there's a particular church I'd like to visit, and I'd like to buy a couple of souvenirs as well."

"How was your day? I was awake and heard you both. Rolf left pretty promptly though." smirked Martha.

"You with your insinuations ... if you aren't a good girl, I won't tell you anything anymore!"

"OK, I'll be quiet, and I can't wait for your account. What did you think of Pelekas?"

"It was simply wonderful."

Once they had arrived in town, Martha was in the pic-ture about everything. The first thing she said about it was: "What? You kissed each other? Then I wasn't wrong about everything my dear!"

"At that moment it just felt right, it just happened, believe me ... if I had had a moment to contemplate it ..."

"Yes, yes, that's what everyone says, who *it* has happened to. But *it* doesn't just happen on its own, we contribute to it. Do you regret it at all?" grinned Martha, with a sly sideways glance.

"No, I don't, because it was quite agreeable."

"Well, at least you are honest."

"Martha!"

"What's the matter? I'm just happy for you. Enjoy it ... and leave the moralizing out of it."

Sophie said nothing for a while.

"Are you angry with me? asked Martha.

"No, how can I be angry with you, you're my friend."

"Good, then let's go shopping and lose no more words over it. But keep me posted, OK?"

Sophie laughed. "Yes, I will, promise."

"There you are, you're smiling again."

"Please show me the Saint Spyridon's church again, I've really got to go there, but on my own."

"Of course, then in the meantime I'll go and have an ice cream, we'll meet up in the Liston."

Within the church, which is located behind the *Café Liston*, are the mortal remains of the saint. In accordance with local traditions, they are paraded out throughout the town four times a year in a procession, accompanied by a multitude of musical ensembles, to celebrate his miracles.

The church of Saint Spyridon was originally built at *Sarocco Square*. However, in 1590 it was relocated to the present position. The architecture of the church is similarly a typical example of Venetian construction style. The bell-tower is the highest point in the town and one of the first landmarks people see, when they approach Corfu by ship.

As Sophie walked closer to the church, she closed her eyes for a moment.

No, it wasn't here, she thought immediately, *but I'm going to go in, because the saint is supposed to be at rest here.*

There were only a few visitors inside, mostly elderly ladies, with their heads bowed in silent prayer.

Sophie approached the tomb of the saint and stood respectfully before it. She had never been a regular churchgoer, she had even left the catholic church a few years ago, but here she was moved by something that was previously unknown to her.

"Did you hear my prayers, so long ago, Saint?" she asked quietly, "I hope you did." She made the sign of the cross and stood still, waiting, as though the saint was going to answer her.

On leaving, she lit two candles. *One for Nikos and one for Helena*, she thought.

After meeting up with Martha at the café, they ordered milky coffees. The waiter also brought them a bottle of water and a plate of small cakes.

"Did you order that?" asked Sophie.

"No," she laughed, "It is customary here."

Once they were back home, Martha asked: "Are you looking forward to tomorrow? You were wanting to go to Kassiopi, weren't you? You'll like it there, there is a very scenic harbour with lots of taverns and cafés."

"Seeing as though I have liked everything so far, it is hardly likely that Kassiopi will be the exception, although I sort of have a funny feeling just thinking about it."

"Why is that then? Do you think you will experience another of your visions there?"

"I don't know, we shall see. Thanks again for the delicious dinner. What was the restaurant called, by the way? I didn't notice its name."

"*Aegli*, we often go there when we are in town, it is so agreeable to sit there under the arcades and observe the people."

CHAPTER 21

The one God divided himself therefore and became two individuals, soul mates and remained nevertheless one whole, one God. The thoughts you have flow freely between you. Your thoughts which manifest themselves as feelings flow between you. You are linked to your soul mate, as though there were a divine elastic band. It can extend itself eternally, yet still remain intact. You are as close to your soul mate as a breath that has been drawn, a moment, a passion. Because you remember: Time, distance and space neither measure nor separate the invisible, do not measure the IS, called LIFE! (Ramtha)

Wednesday

During the period of the Roman occupation after 230 BC, Kassiopi was, after *Kerkyra,* the next most important town on Corfu. The first historical recording was made by Cicero, who lived there for seven days in 48 B.C. It was recorded that the Emperor Nero visited *Kassiopi* in the year 67 A.D. and in honour of the father of the Gods, sang a song to the sanctity of Zeus in the vicinity of the present *Panagia-Kassopitra-Church.* Emperor Tiberius is even supposed to have owned a residence there.

Taverns, bars, mini-markets and souvenir shops line the road to the attractive harbour. Boats offering day trips wait for their passengers and it is also possible to rent out small motorboats. The view of Albania, on the opposite side across the narrow straits, drives home its major strategic significance of former times.

The whole of the Mediterranean suffered from piracy and the kidnapping of European coastal citizens. The harbour at *Kassiopi*, in its protected cove, has a particular charm. There are almost always sailing boats or motorized yachts anchored in the harbour. Fishing boats on the other hand are now scarce.

On their way to the harbour they drove through an alley which was paved with large flagstones. They found a parking space and Sophie got out of the car in order to take photos.

"It is so picturesque! Rolf, thank you for showing it to me. Have you already taken photos here?"

"Funnily enough, no, not yet, I don't know why, but either I had left my equipment at home, or the light wasn't right on that day. But today I have it with me, it is just the smaller set, but it should be sufficient. May I also take a couple of photos of you later? I've been wanting to ask you for a couple of days now."

"If you promise not to post them on Instagram, then yes, you can."

"I promise, they're just for us. In that case, I'll take my camera with me, I'm sure we will find other attractive motives too."

"And today I have brought my bathing things, so that something like when we were at the White House won't happen again."

Rolf had been to this place many times, but what he now experienced here, he would never forget. The water seemed to call out to him and cast a spell over him.

He watched a proud sailing boat set sail and from the end of the pier, a woman with long brown hair waved it goodbye.

A short time later, he had the sad confirmation of how his earlier life almost certainly had ended.

They had hardly gone more than a few steps, when he suddenly came to a stop and began to weep bitterly. She embraced him and there they stood, in the midst of the tourists' curious stares.

The sun rises behind swirling fountains of sand, high over the horizon, as he forces himself through the crowds of people on the quay of Kassiopi, who jostle about whilst the preparations are being made for the ships to put out to sea and new crews are hired. However today, the unrest is particularly great. The hot south wind had blown in overnight.

Seagulls were screeching over the harbour, diving down now and again to pluck scraps out of the water.

He saunters down the harbour pier and observes the wide berthed ships, which are lined up next to each other waiting for their freight or disembark goods. He has often been here, but today he is excited.

Today he wants to ... he must get hired, if he wants to get to Venice in order to seek his fortune. In the eyes of the Goddess Athena they were already married, but only then would he be able to officially marry Helena. A large, bearded man approaches him, just when he was about to turn away in disappointment.

"Are you looking for work?" he asks in a mixture of French and Greek. Intuitively Nikos understands the question ... that is the reason he is here." The bearded man reeks of sweat and brandy, but he points to a ship. A ship that doesn't seem to correspond to the man's appearance.

With wide eyes he beheld the three-master brig, with its three, brilliant white, trapeze-shaped square sails of the full-rigged foremast and mizzen, and the mainmast with an extra red and white mainsail, fluttering in the gentle breeze. He estimates the ship to be at least ninety feet long and thirty feet wide. Above the upper topgallant sail, a light blue flag flies atop what has to be a one hundred and twenty foot high mainmast. This depicts three flying albatrosses, one red, one blue and one green. Just below, the boatswain's chair rotates, quietly creaking languidly in the wind. Even the iron anchor chain has a matt shine in the sunlight. The shackles are exemplary polished and the sight of them would please even the strictest of captains. Cork fenders hang over the railing and the fender ropes are loosely thrown over them. *It is quite obvious that the captain runs a tight ship*, he thought, *even if he looks terrible himself.* This ship stands out a mile from the other sailing boats and freight boats.

He feels very small standing next to this proud ship. On the broad sides, where the name *Héroine* was stencilled in gold lettering, there are three large rescue boats, whose oarlocks also have a matt shine. The gangway has been lowered, two thick ropes serve as handrails. Men are carrying supplies on board and rolling water barrels up the narrow walkway.

"We need someone for the galley, a new cook. Maurice took off yesterday. Can you cook?" he emphasizes his spoken words with gestures and Nikos understands his meaning also. He nods. He will sail to Venice on this ship.

"Come back in two days, at the eleventh hour we set sail. Be punctual, we won't wait for you. However, if Maurice shows up again, the deals off."

He should have been happy about this piece of news, but he leaves the harbour with drooping shoulders, his hardest task ahead of him.

He is lucky, fate looks fairly upon him, for Maurice did not return.

It has been three days now since they set sail and he has now got his sea legs.

The wind, which now only fills the sails of the main-mast and the aft lateen sail, pushes the Spaniard - as the captain said – around and into the wind.

That was the moment when the *Héroine*, which had already turned into the wind, shot past the starboard side of the Spaniard with her expiring drive. Her sails were clewed up, the square sails braced, fore and aft.

The men of the boarding party throw grappling hooks over, the bodies of both ships collide into each other side on side, screams, curses and shots sound.

"Onwards!" screams the captain. "Onwards men! Give it the Dons! On her!"

Then several canons roar out of the belly of the galle-on. It was to be the last sound in his life, that Nikos ever heard. Then there is only water, the infinite deep, and his last thoughts, '*Helena*'.

CHAPTER 22

You think I'm holding back knowledge from you? I do. Do you know why? Because you can't cope with everything. Many things you are not willing to know because you are still looking to the future with a suspicious, fearful mindset.
Until you can make a change from boredom to happiness, you are not ready to know everything that will happen. (Ramtha)

After ten minutes Rolf had just about composed himself again. They walked slowly, hand in hand and sat down on a bench. Her gaze wandered from there to the Albanian mountains. Small colourful boats rocked in the water right in front of them, children fed schools of fish with bread and further out, three sailing boats had cast anchor. Sophie suddenly pointed to the end of the dock.

"I have to go there now, can I leave you alone?"

"Yes, you can, I'll wait here and take some photos in the meantime."

She ran to the entrance of the harbour and sat herself down on a pile of large coarsely hewn stones, which were probably due to be used for the expansion of the pier. Here, she was alone. She thought about the vision Rolf had just told her and her heart became heavy.

Saint Spiridon didn't answer their prayers.

Maybe she hadn't prayed enough, or earlier in Kerkyra she should have lit many more candles at the coffin of the saint. However, she was not allowed to go back to town after she had embarrassed the noble and rich Alexios, the man whom her father had chosen for her to marry.

Spiros, the trusted friend and Kleitos the large sheepdog, accompany her. His donkey is packed with several belongings, firewood and food in order to live for some time in hiding. He leads a goat on a rope, because she will need the milk. Spiros has vowed not to betray her, but she believes him without the oath. Every two days he will come and check on her and bring her food.

At the end of Loutses they go steeply uphill. They silently follow the narrow path until it ends. From there they continue through thick bushes until a small trampled path can be seen, which comes out at the end of a valley.

The path descends steeply and is full of stones and roots. As it has rained a few days earlier, the descent is slippery. Spiro worriedly urges caution.

In her arms, she hold the most precious thing she possesses, her child. Nikos' child, to whom she gave his name. She gave birth alone in Spiros' house. She has been waiting for news from Venice for many moons. Once a week, Spiros asks the sailors who cast anchor in Kassiopi. But no one has ever heard of Nikos. They were already a couple. The old shaman Sofia, whom her grandmother had had brought over from the mainland, had married them in the grotto of Afionas before the goddess Athena. Only Spiros and her Yaya were present as witnesses. After the ceremony, her grandmother had given a small banquet.

When they said goodbye, they had hugged each other for a long time. "Beloved Yaya, I will never forget that."

"I loved doing this for you, my dear little Helena," and to Nikos she had said, "You take good care of my granddaughter, do you hear?"

"That I'll promise you, by the Gods!" he had answered, and embraced her in his arms also.

The further they go down the path, the louder the birds' noise becomes. Countless crow-like birds shoot out of the rock face that towers above them on the left-hand side. The echo of the birds screeching increases the racket that the birds are creating. Then they stand in front of the entrance to a cave.

Hardly anyone knows of this place. By chance, Spiros had heard about it from an old shepherd, who had used it to shelter his flock during storms. The cave had a wide entrance and seemed to be very deep.

Spiros lights a torch, gives it to her and takes one himself. The cave is damp, sometimes drops of moisture fall from the ceiling.

Spiros stops the donkey and unpacks its load.

"He has to stay here, it is too dangerous, we have to go a little deeper inside," said Spiro, "It's drier there."

Apparently, the cave is inhabited by the crow-like birds, which have their nests all around, in which they raise their young. Then it goes almost vertically downwards. Presently it leads over large rocks and down a short way. She holds her child anxiously in her arms. She would never forgive herself if something were to happen to her son.

Then they arrived.

"Here it is," Spiros points to an area of about ten paces in diameter. It is dry and warmer than at the entrance to the cave. In the middle there is a cold fireplace and on one side of the room she sees a simple sleeping area.

"No one will find you here, Helena, you are safe. It won't be long. In three days, my friend Aris returns from Venice, he will surely bring good news."

"I'm scared Spiros, Nikos has been gone for such a long time."

Her friend takes her in his arms, after she has laid her son down on the bed of straw. He is screaming because he is hungry.

"Don't be afraid, you have to hope for the best."

"Oh, Spiros I'd so love to."

Then she gave the little Nikos his milk, whilst Spiros lights a fire. A short while later her son falls asleep with a satisfied smile.

Three days later, she received the sad confirmation, when Spiros visits her in the cave. In due course, she had even settled in a little. Every day at noon, she went outside in the sun with her son for a few hours. Laughing she had watched Nikos crawling around in the grass, trying to catch butterflies. Kleitos, the gentle bodyguard, was always in his presence. Those were the moments during which she could forget her pain. She would never be able to return home, never see her parents again, never go back to her old gnarled olive tree, no matter what happened.

"Spiros, what is the matter?" she asks, when she sees his sad face. "Do you have any news?"

"Yes, I have ... and I am so sorry ..."

She immediately began to cry, after a while she said: "Tell me everything. Little Nikos is still asleep, so we have time."

Spiros reached for her hand and held it tight.

"I had already found out that Nikos was taken on as ships' cook on a ship called *Héroine*.

"Yesterday, I was in the harbours pub having a meal and by chance I overheard a conversation at the neighbouring table.

A man with a scarred face was bragging about working as a gunner on a Spanish warship. He had boasted about the fact that it wasn't recognisable as a warship, in order to mislead the pirates. One day, they really were attacked by pirates. It was the *Héroine*. They had sunk the ship, lock, stock and barrel."

Now they were both in tears, the faithful friend and the young widow.

"He signed up on a pirate ship?" she asks, finally.

"I'm sure that he didn't know that, Nikos wouldn't have dreamed of doing that ... no matter how much he wanted to get to Venice."

"Of course not," she sobbed loudly, "What am I going to do now?"

He thought for a moment.

"I can take you to your grandmother in Afionas in two days if you wish."

"Thank you, my friend, you have always been so good to us, I don't know how I can ever thank you."

"I must go, Helena, otherwise people in the village will be asking themselves why I leave my workshop alone for so long."

"Yes of course ... we shall see each other again in two days."

Shortly after Spiros has left, she knows what she will do. Very early the next morning she will take the child into town, slip into the stable and leave it with a message. After the initial shock, his grandparents will surely take loving care of the little Nikos.

Then she will take a donkey and ride to the harbour at Kassiopi.

CHAPTER 23

Well, what is the voice of God? What is that knowledge that you believed would come from heaven like a flash of lightning to tell you what to do? They are feelings, the voice of God are feelings. To listen to the voice of God implies you listen to what you feel. In feeling is in fact, the unspeakable knowledge. Now you understand why I cannot teach you that knowledge, because you are the ones who must feel it! I can tell you about the feeling, but you will never understand what I am talking about until you experience it, until you feel it. Do you understand now? (Ramtha)

What is she doing now? thought Rolf, in astonishment.

He looked through the telephoto lens of his camera and was terrified. Sophie was standing up to her hips in water and was openly crying. Her brown hair was flying in the wind and then she hid her face in her hands. The loud signal horn of a large motorboat, full of tourists, tore her out of her reverie. On board, there was loud music playing and people's laughter rang out. Some were dancing on the deck.

She turned around and saw Rolf, with his camera in his hand, sitting on the bench.

"What flavour was that?" she asked, on returning to him in her soaking wet trousers and discovered the cardboard cup of ice cream that had almost completely melted.

"Mint and caramel, you can get it over here. I'll go and get you one too, if you like."

"That is a good idea, I could really do with one right now. But beforehand I have to dry myself off and put a different pair of trousers on. It's a good job that I have brought a spare pair with me. I'm beginning to get cold in these jeans. Could I have the car key please?"

She returned ten minutes later. Now she was wearing white shorts.

"Were you crying just now? I saw you sitting there, but I didn't want to disturb you. You must have been gone for an hour. Why did you go into the water? You scared the life out of me!"

I'm so sorry, but I had to do it. I'm back again now."

She gave him a kiss on the cheek.

"I didn't realise at all, that it was such a long time."

"I know. You lose all track of time. Do you want to talk about it?"

"Yes, I'll tell you about it, but first that ice cream, OK?"

"Of course, a couple of minutes won't make any difference ... It is lovely to see you smile, I like that." He was silent for a few minutes and watched an old fisherman repair a net, whilst Sophie ate her ice cream.

"I now know why I had to go to the pier, but one thing at a time. Anyway, you were right, we were married, previously."

"I told you."

But you didn't see it, did you? I know it now, though."

"And?"

"We were married by a shaman, that my grandmother had fetched ... and she married us in a grotto, somewhere in the vicinity of her home, in a ceremony in the presence of the Goddess Athena. Only Spiros and my Yaya were there as witnesses."

"Then it can only possibly be the grotto behind the double bay, that's where one is. You have to climb a bit, but I've been there already."

"I'd like to go there."

"Really?"

"Yes, do you want come along?"

"Of course, but we won't manage it anymore today, because it will be dark by them."

"Then on Saturday, that's my last day. Tomorrow is the party at Martha's. Will you be there?"

"Of course I'm coming. It is your names-day. Shall we stay here and go out for dinner?"

"That's a good idea, then we can have a look around town. I'm quite curious to see what has changed since then." she smiled.

Later they were sitting in *Janis Taverne,* which is right on the harbour, drinking white wine and sharing prawns in tomato sauce.

Sophie pointed to the end of the pier.

"That is where I went into the water ... then."

"What a kind of love that must have been, Sophie."

"Yes, it was. I want to drink to the health of Helena and Nikos." They raised their glasses, drained them and kissed each other.

"Didn't you want to ...?"

"Yes, that's what I wanted ... but if it doesn't suit here, then where? Now be quiet and kiss me again."

After a few minutes silence, Rolf said quietly: "Such a sad, yet lively place."

They gazed out to sea, where the setting of the sun bathed the mountains in an orange light.

"I have to tell you something else, I couldn't say it before."

She took his hand.

"I've gone very dizzy all of a sudden, wait a moment, I need a drink of water first."

"Feeling better?"

"Yes, I think I know it already, but ... we had a child, didn't we?

Then her eyes filled with tears once again.

"Yes, a son ... I called him Nikos ... but I think he was alright. I brought him to my parents, before I ... oh, well, you know."

"I'm sure they looked after him very well."

"I think so too ... and his grandfather most certainly made sure that he was successful in life."

"Come on, let's go, it's on me."

Via *Avliotes*, *Roda*, and *Sidari* they drove through the village of *Kavadades*.

"But I know this place! Isn't that Mon Amour? Why are you turning off? You have to drive straight on for Arillas, don't you?"

"No, I don't, Sophie, I live here."

They didn't speak a word until he opened the door to his house.

"You live very nicely here," said Sophie, after he had shown her everything. "Are they your parents?"

She pointed to a wall with tastefully framed photographs hanging on it.

He took her by the hand and led her to the photos.

"These are my parents, on the left are all my grandparents ... By the way, that is the grandfather, to whom I have to thank for this house ... then there is a lovely photo of my sister ... and in this one ..."

"... you are with Mia." Sophie added.

"That's right, her brother took it. It shows us dancing at the wedding. Fortunately, it wasn't videoed, I felt so sorry for Mia, I've no idea just how often I trod on her feet!" laughed Rolf, "Come out onto the terrace, it's such a beautiful night. There's a new moon. You could travel to the stars, just look. Perhaps our son is somewhere up there, looking down on us. It is said that every soul has a star."

Sophie came up behind him and embraced him.

"What a wonderful thought," she whispered. "Maybe he is back on earth though, just like us. As Martha, for example, who knows?"

"That's another lovely thought, she got us together, after all."

"That's exactly what I mean."

"I'll get us some wine and a blanket. It is cooler here that in the valley."

And so they sat at length, drinking, laughing and crying together. Time and time again, they experienced memories from their common past life together.

At some point Rolf looked at the clock.

"It's half past one Sophie. May I make a wish?"

"You don't need to, I'm staying tonight here with you."

CHAPTER 24

You can talk to your companion through feelings and ask the being to share knowledge with you. The being will absorb that feeling and may be driven to go to a certain place, because the feeling draws it there. Have you ever felt the urge to do something? Often this is because your companion wants to know something. And so you go, have the experience and you say: "Now I know." But in the meantime your companion says: "Wonderful! I can feel it! And if I can feel it, I possess the wisdom of it!" (Ramtha)

Thursday

"Drop me off here please, I don't want to wake anyone up. At seven o'clock some are most certainly still asleep."

They kissed their goodbyes and Rolf whispered in her ear: "Thank you for the unforgettable night."

"I thank you too ... but we have to leave it at that, you know that. It was Helena and Nikos' night."

Rolf didn't reply, just kissed her again.

She closed the car door quietly and sneaked down the narrow path through the olive grove to her apartment, like a child, who doesn't want to get caught. Once there, she sat on the bed and cried.

Two hours left to sleep, she thought, *and then the party, too. Let's see how long I last.*

Contrary to her expectations, she felt rested after getting up. She showered and dressed.

"How can I help you, Martha?"

"Oh, it's good that you're here, love. I didn't hear you come home at all, you weren't at home, you were at Rolf's, weren't you? You certainly haven't slept much!"

"Well, there's no fooling you!" grinned Sophie.

"And?"

"What, 'and?' It was lovely Martha ... but it was a one-off situation and had more to do with our past lives ... I now see you in a different light though." she smiled."

"What do you mean?"

"I'll tell you later, so just tell me what I should do."

"Grandma isn't feeling very well, so now we have to muck in. Could you like to peel the potatoes? I'll finish doing the salad, and you can tell me everything ... look at all this."

"Sure, I'll do it ... to both. What is going on?"

"Kostas is already in the courtyard and is starting the fire, he wants to grill a lamb on a spit. You really must try the innards, everyone always very keen on having some. I'll go and tell him to save you some in a minute. Before that, there is a type of rice soup with egg, a speciality from here, then of course there is a load of grilled meat. Chicken, fish, pork, I assure you, that you will never have seen so much food on one table before!"

"He shouldn't go to so much trouble, I'm not going to starve ... I'll go and congratulate him then, he'll get his present after the meal."

"You have a present? Oh, he will be pleased about that, what is it?"

"Just a T-shirt. I discovered it in town and found it quite funny. I hope you had a present for him too." laughed Sophie.

"Of course, I've given it to him already though."

"Are you going to tell me what it is?"

"Sure, he probably won't hear you later, because he's wearing his new iPhone headphones, he is an absolute Apple fan and has been wanting to have some for ages. I have a little something for you too."

"For me?"

"Sure ... don't you have your names-day too today? ... somehow?"

Sophie smiled: "In a sense, yes ... that you thought of that too."

"You think that your story doesn't move me? Especially since what you found out about yesterday. If you have finished doing the potatoes, you can help me lay the table."

"Just tell me what you want me to do, I'm up to it."

"I can't believe that your holiday is over in two days. The time has flown by."

"Tell me about it! I can still see myself as I arrived on the first day, pale and worn out."

"Plenty has happened since then, hasn't it?"

"You can say that again! If someone had told me that beforehand, I wouldn't have believed them ... I would have probably ... no, *definitely* not boarded the aeroplane."

"That bad?"

"No, Martha, so unbelievably wonderful, but at the same time, scary."

"All the same, you fell in love."

"I wouldn't call it that, no. If you had asked me two weeks ago, whether you can love two men at the same time, I would have vehemently denied it. I love Michael and I love Rolf, especially because he was Nikos."

"And what are you going to do about it?"

"What am I going to do about it? I am going to leave it here. Martha, you know my life in Muenster, and you know that I would never, ever, give up my work. Michael is in Kiel, he is my partner. I have my friends in Germany and my family ..."

"I had all that too, Sophie."

"Yes, I know, but we're different, dear, it's important for me to have control over my life. Here, it was different. Oh well, let's leave it at that for now. I am looking forward to the party."

It was a fantastic celebration. The first guests already arrived at one o'clock in the afternoon and the last ones left at one o'clock in the morning. Even little Maria stayed up late and her grandmother also managed to stay until the end of the party.

She even danced with Kostas. Martha was right, Sophie had never seen so much food before and she couldn't remember the names of the numerous guests.

Early in the evening, Rolf arrived. After he had congratulated Kostas, he hugged Sophie.

"Happy names-day, Helena, here, this is for you."

He handed her a cardboard tube.

"What is it?"

"Have a look inside and see for yourself."

Sophie opened the lid and extracted a large, rolled up, glossy colour photograph.

"Oh, how wonderful! I never even noticed!"

"Long distance lens," he smiled, "Perhaps that's why it turned out so well, because you didn't notice ... I hope you like it as much as I do."

At that moment Martha came over and observed the photo.

"Wow, that is a terrific picture of you, is it from yesterday?"

"Yes," answered Rolf, "That was after she had got changed ... I expect you've heard that Sophie went into the water fully clothed. I shot the photo as she came out of the restaurant she had changed in."

"Hey, not in the restaurant, in the toilets!" laughed Sophie.

"I have another little something for you," he pulled a small object wrapped in colourful paper out of his jacket pocket, "But you aren't to open it until this evening, when you go to bed."

Dead tired, Sophie fell into bed at two o'clock in the morning, then she remembered the little present from Rolf. She unwrapped it carefully.

It was a small white dog, with black patches around his eyes.

"Hello Kleitos." She whispered, and pressing it to her heart she fell asleep, weeping.

CHAPTER 25

If you learn to apply science, then it may be that you and your soul mate begin to attract each other; you meet in the middle, at the point that is called "being." To reach the state of IS, from being, means complete acceptance of the whole God with your whole being. The more conscious you are of your other self, the closer you get in expressing yourselves, because you share energy experiences. (Ramtha)

Friday

Rolf picked her up at midday. "Did you sleep well, Sophie?"

"Until just now," she laughed. "Do you realise how tired I was?"

"I can imagine. I'm sure you stayed up longer than I did."

"With me it was after two o'clock."

"Then it was longer. You know, you are wearing the same outfit that you wore on your first day, when I picked you up."

"You've noticed that? You're right, I was allowed to use Martha's washing machine."

"I'm a photographer, forgotten already?" he laughed.

"Of course not. Do you realise how happy you made me ... with the dog?"

"Not with the photo?" he grinned.

"That too, but I think you were aware of that already."

"Where did you get the little Kleitos? Can you buy them here?"

"No, I don't think so, maybe in town. Yours belonged to my collection. I used to have a soft spot for model animals from *Schleich,* have you heard of them*?"*

"Yes, our children's ward have several of them. They are really very well made, but I didn't recall seeing any in your house."

"Because these days I keep them in a box."

"In any case you scored a bullseye with it, thank you."

"I'm glad about that, and Kleitos is sure to be happy about the change of scenery."

They both laughed.

"So, where are we going?"

"I'll show you a beautiful path and an even more beautiful bay, let me surprise you."

Of the many coastal landscapes on Corfu, the northernmost one is perhaps the most beautiful. It is accessible within about thirty minutes on foot by a countryside trail. Beginning at the primary school at *Peruládes*, initially there is a gentle ascent, then it slopes down to the sea and suddenly you have the panorama of the bay before you. Below the approximately one hundred metre high towering cape, sandstone formations have created a bay, in front of which a small island lies.

Hand in hand, they walked down the path, which snakes its way past the cape, until they reached the tiny bay surrounded by flat rocks. They were completely alone.

"Let's go swimming, Sophie, the sea is calm, and we can easily get to the water from the little sandy beach."

"It's crystal clear, how wonderful, but I haven't anything with me."

"So what? I've already seen you naked, come on in!"

He stripped off and ran into the water.

After swimming, they lay on the beach and let themselves dry off the sun.

"It is so beautiful here," said Sophie, later. They had dressed and were watching the seagulls drawing great circles in the sky. "I could do with something to eat ... my God, I'm sure you must take me for a glutton! I'm always eating!

He laughed. "Why? It is nearly evening and anyway That's the good sea air. I'll take you to Seventh Heaven now."

She looked at him sceptically. "Remember what we agreed on."

"Ha-ha, in this case, the 'Seventh Heaven' is the name of a restaurant, just up there on the hill, so you have nothing to worry about ... aside of a panoramic view and tasty things to eat."

"Good! I can go with that!" she smiled.

Later they were sitting on one of the swinging chairs from which they had an almost Caribbean view over the sea.

"This is a lovely idea, totally relaxing, as if I wasn't already. Could I try a bit of your burger? You can have some of my mussels."

"They taste very good, the mussels. I think I'll order them next time too. ..."

"When you'll be sitting here without me ..."

"Please don't remind me of that, Sophie. Are you already thinking about your departure?"

"Yes, but not often, not so much about the departure, but about that which comes afterwards. Especially, of how Michael will react, when I tell him all about it."

"Everything?"

"Yes, it's only fair, don't you think?"

"I'm not very sure, to tell you the truth. What will it change? How would you like it, if the shoe was on the other foot?"

"Pretty awful, I suppose."

"You see. I think something like that is worse for men, than it is for women, you are more tolerant. Probably has something to do with ancient territorial instincts. Is he a jealous type?"

"Yes, a little, but isn't that normal, when you love someone?"

"I've thought about it a lot and I've now come to the conclusion, that it has something to do with an inferiority complex."

"Inferiority complex?"

"Yes, you're afraid that someone else is better than you."

Sophie contemplated that for a while and sipped her orange juice.

"That could be true, I'll have to have a think about that. So, you think it would be better not to tell Michael about our night together?"

"That is something that you have to decide ... I wouldn't."

So they sat for a while, in silence and enjoyed the view.

"I'm dead tired," said Sophie, "Can you drive me home? I've got to get an hour's sleep. We could go out again later."

"Out for dinner?"

"Funny guy," she laughed, "But then again, why not? You know what ... you never mentioned anything about your old school friend, the one you wanted to meet up with."

"Oh, yes, I had a good time. He has a lovely wife. Unfortunately, they only had a couple of hours to spare, because they had to re-embark. I couldn't imagine him ever going on a cruise before. It was supposedly more her decision, but he was obviously enjoying it too. What didn't please him, was the thought of having put on what felt like a hundred kilos. The food must really be very good on such a ship. They were calling at five more ports, they must be in Cairo by now. So, one gets around. It's not my cup of tea though. What about you?"

"I'm not sure, maybe when I'm retired. My parents have become real cruise junkies. I think they have travelled halfway around the world."

"Are you scared of heights?" Something had just occurred to him, "Can you see the glass terrace over there?"

"Yes, I'd like to go over there, come on!"

"Then let's go, I'll just get the camera out of the car."

"I bet this is a major challenge for people who are scared of heights. You get the impression you're standing in mid-air!"

"That's why I asked. Lots of people don't dare to come here. Wait a sec., I'll take a couple of photos of you."

"But no Instagram!"

"I promise, they're only for us."

CHAPTER 26

Soul mates have embarked on this puzzle, called life, for the purpose of expression, for the purpose of the experience of unrestricted sensation. Their journey into a three dimensional plane was not for the purpose of finding each other. Because they were already one another. Their wish and desire was to experience the picture and to be a part of it. (Ramtha)

Saturday

"It was really enjoyable yesterday evening in Akrotiri, particularly because Martha and Kostas joined us. I had a bad conscience at first because I have done so little with Martha."

"The way I see it, you don't need to have one."

"I know that now, she doesn't begrudge me my experience. I told her everything, by the way. Should I have asked for your permission?"

"I was aware that she knows. No, you are a free person, of course you can tell your best friend everything."

"The most beautiful was the sunset, which we saw from the roof. But the whole atmosphere in Akrotiri is very relaxed, along with the beautiful music, the friendly people ... I can understand why belongs to one of you regular haunts."

"There are three, actually," said Rolf, "The Gravia, the Ammos and the Akrotiri."

"A very good choice. You really do have good taste."

"Look at you, Sophie."

"You old charmer."

"It is only the truth. Would you still like to visit the grotto?"

Sophie thought for a moment.

"Yes, I would, you don't want to?"

"Well, if I am quite honest with you, I do have my doubts."

"Doubts? Why?"

"Because I think it could get very emotional again ... so close to your departure."

"I, ... We'll manage it, Rolf. I have the feeling that it will round off our story somehow and that it will be easier for me to depart. Don't you think?"

"You might be right there, Sophie, alright then, we'll climb ... but before that, there's the highlight that I wanted to keep until your last day."

"Another one? Up until now, there's been nothing but highlights!"

"But it's very special. You should bring your good appetite with you."

Sophie laughed out loud: "Well that's shouldn't be a problem! At home my scales are going to go off the range and I'll need a new white coat for in the clinic!"

"Now you are exaggerating, I don't see any difference."

"Because you see me through different eyes, my dear. Can you take your camera with you later?"

"It has been in the car since Kassiopi"

"Ooh, my God, you really didn't exaggerate," Sophie marvelled when they arrived at the *Fisherman's Cabin* restaurant at noon. "The way through the olive groves was incredibly beautiful, like going through a fairy tale forest. In a different type of car that could've been quite difficult."

"The path is a part of it, if it were to be developed, it wouldn't be the same. During the season I come here almost every week. But don't get annoyed by Kostas, the landlord, he can be grumpy, but he is actually quite friendly, if he likes someone. *The Fisherman's* is a real family business too. Mother and son cook, father and daughter wait on. She's very pretty, by the way."

"I see, that is the reason why you come here so often." she smiled mischievously.

"Wait and see."

"The colours! My word, that is really Greece, this blue ... and right on the waterfront. That is so romantic!" Sophie was delighted.

Only two of the tables were occupied, apparently the guests had come on foot.

"It will fill up later," said Rolf, "Shall we sit there? Then we will have a little shade."

Kostas came up to the table and greeted them both. He brought a plate with three raw fish.

"These are just your thing, eh Rolf, what do you think? Red snapper, monkfish and a dorado. They were caught with a harpoon, you'll notice that by their taste, because they didn't die stressfully in a net. Would you like them?

"Shall we?" asked Rolf.

"Alright, we'll take them."

"Then we'll take the red snapper and the monkfish."

Rolf mobile rang and he took the call.

"Yes, you can set off, we have just ordered our meal, thank you for doing that for us, my friend."

"Another highlight?" asked Sophie, after he had terminated the call.

"It's a surprise."

"I think that was the best fish, that I have ever eaten." stated Sophie after the meal.

"I'm glad, then I didn't get your expectations up too high, after all."

"No, not at all, it was simply delicious."

"Right, I'll go and pay, I'll be back in a moment."

In the meantime, Sophie took a few photos.

"Now you have to try this."

"What is it?"

"Home-made limoncello. Here you get one free of charge, when you pay the bill."

"I know that from Italy," Sophie sipped from the glass. "This is really good. Delicious."

"Are you ready, Sophie?"

"Ready for what?"

"For a short ride in a boat."

"A boat ride? Now?"

"Yes, I think Aristides has just arrived. Give me your hand. He'll be down there in a moment."

"Where are we going?" asked Sophie, when they were seated in the small motorboat and had been greeted my Aristides with a wide smile.

"We are saving ourselves the climbing and the many bathers in the double bay. Aristides is taking us directly to the grotto. Thanks, my friend, for you doing this for us."

"It's my pleasure," replied the landlord from the Graziella.

Ten minutes later, the boat was rolling gently on the tide at the lower entrance to the grotto.

"Do you want to get out?" asked Aristides.

"Yes, please." said Sophie.

"But be careful," he warned, "The rocks are very slippery."

"Give me your hand, Sophie, I'll go first."

Before, we came from up there, over the steep scree slope."

"You know that now?"

"I can see it very clearly right now," said Sophie, in a strangled voice, "You carried my grandmother down here on your back."

A little later they sat, hand in hand on a rock on the inside of the grotto. Aristides had steered the boat a short distance out of the bay and switched its motor off. Perhaps he perceived how important this moment was for the two of them.

Rolf had closed his eyes.

"In the middle was the fire that Spiros had lit, I can see it, as though it was burning right here, right now. He had carried the wood the whole, long way here."

"I can even see it without closing my eyes ... it is unbelievable!"

"You looked very beautiful with the crown of flowers in your hair.

"I can smell the aroma of sage and other herbs in my nose..."

"... The old shaman ignited them."

After a quarter of an hour, Sophie said: "Come on, let's go, it was important and very beautiful being here, I thank you." She gave him a kiss and in that moment they were Helena and Nikos, once again. They drove back through the olive groves to Arillas in silence.

"I'd like to have our last drink in the Ammos, that's where we met for the first time."

"That is a very good idea, we'll do that."

"Shall we share the prawn dish? They look very tasty." she asked, as they were sitting in the Ammos.

"Are you already hungry?"

"No not hungry, but I could do with something all the same, lunch was already hours ago," she pointed to the neighbouring table," Can you resist prawns? I can't!"

"Then I'll order a salad as well, because I'm probably not going to get many of the prawns. But tomorrow, I can eat a whole portion for myself."

"Now that was mean!"

"I'm sorry, but I'm afraid the only thing to help me at the moment is sarcasm. The fact that you will be gone tomorrow is hard for me to take."

"It isn't easy for me either, believe me, that's why we should just enjoy the last few hours. Look at how beautiful the light looks over the sea. Give me your hand."

After the meal, they sat closely entwined and observed the lively antics on the street.

When Rolf settled the bill with Leo in the pub later, he said: "You see, I was right."

"Yes, you clairvoyant," laughed Rolf.

"I think I'd better go to bed," said Sophie, "I've got a strenuous day ahead of me tomorrow. Will you drive me? I can walk too, though."

"Of course I'll drive you."

"Thanks for not asking whether we can spend my last night together at your house."

"I must admit, it was hard."

"I know." she gave him a kiss on the cheek. "Sleep well ... and be punctual tomorrow, do you hear me?"

CHAPTER 27

Well, soul mates share their experiences with each other. Consequently you are not only enriched by the elements of your incarnations on this plane, but you profit from the shared wisdom of your other self, who has also become an individual, just like you yourselves are one. There was a reason: Love. (Ramtha)

Sunday

As promised, Rolf called round at Martha and Kostas' house after he had taken Sophie to the airport. They were sitting on the terrace enjoying a glass of wine that Kostas' father had made himself.

"Long ago, I mean a *really* long time ago," perused Kostas, holding his wine glass up to the light, "The wine from Corfu must have been far superior to how it is today, before there were so many olive trees here. Thanks to the Venetians, there are over five million of them on the island. It's said that they have changed the climate. It's cooler and more damp now, and this is supposed to have affected the quality of the grapes."

"I didn't know that," said Rolf, taking a sip of his wine. "I like it nonetheless."

Suddenly, he had to laugh out loud.

"What are you laughing about?" asked Martha.

"Because of his t-shirt!" He pointed to Kostas and read out loud. "Please don't interrupt me when I'm ignoring you."

Martha joined in his laughter. "That was Sophie's name-day present to him. She really did rediscover her humour while she was here."

"I really appreciated it," replied Kostas. "Simply brilliant!"

"How was your parting?"

"Hmm ... intense, Martha ... and tearful, for both of us."

"And ... are you hopeful?"

"Driving back from the airport, a quote from the film "*The Shawshank Redemption*" came to mind. Someone had said *"Hope can really kill a man."* Mind you, it was a prisoner who was behind bars for more than 30 years. I think he was called Red and was played by Morgan Freeman."

"Now that you mention it," said Kostas. "That is one of my all-time favourite films. It was on television again not so long ago, I must have seen it at least five times ... this Red said something else too. When he was released, he changed his mind about it and said:

'*Hope is a good thing, maybe the best of things and no good thing ever dies.*' Freeman received an Oscar nomination for his part but unfortunately it was the same year that Forrest Gump was nominated and in the end Tom Hanks received the award."

"He knows his films, Rolf! No-one is better than him at that!" laughed Martha.

"But all the same, I am not going to delude myself, because we both agreed, that that which happened here, remains here and in our hearts."

"Somehow, it has turned a full circle," observed Martha. "You picked her up from the airport and brought her back to it."

"You're right," Rolf raised his glass. "Dearest Martha, I thank you from the bottom of my heart. It was thanks to knowing you, that I made Sophie's acquaintance."

Martha smiled. "Maybe I was your son. That is what Sophie said to me when she left."

"Maybe, Martha, who knows? I'd like to drink to Sophie's health with you."

"And what are you going to do now?" asked Martha, after they had finished their wine.

"I'm going to start working again tomorrow, the Japanese are waiting."

"And I'm going to go to the little chapel on the cape and place two stones for the pair of you with your four names. There, where Mia's and Alexander's stones lie."

Rolf rose out of his seat, gave Martha a long embrace and whispered *'thank you'* into her ear.

CHAPTER 28

Look at each other. You are wonderful beings and you are well worth the message. You have only just started to contemplate the gloriousness that you embody. I can see it; you have only just started to feel it. If the world were to be as you are, what a wonderful place it would be! Indeed! (Ramtha)

Sophie wept for the full duration of the two hour return flight and the last two weeks played though her mind in all their detail, all over again. She held the little white dog that Rolf had given her the whole time in her hand.

When she finally landed in Hanover, she had let Rolf go.

Michael was waiting for her at the gate with a large bouquet of red roses.

"I am so glad you are back Sophie, these last two weeks have been so damned long!"

"I found they went like wind, but I'm also glad to be back too."

"Yeah, well, I bet you got up to a little more than me."

"Yes, you're probably right ... no, actually you are definitely right. Your idea about not being in touch for a week was a good one, although I was sad at the time."

"Do you think I felt any differently? You look fantastic, suntanned and relaxed ... I look pale in comparison. Give me your case, the car is in the car park, it isn't far, and I have made a reservation for later ... at one of your favourite restaurants, or should I have asked? I even managed to get a table on the terrace."

"No, no everything is just fine, I'm pleased ... and in fact I could actually do with something to eat. I'll start my diet tomorrow."

"Why? I don't think you have put on any weight."

We are going to 'Freiheit 26', how apt, she mused. *A romance author couldn't have chosen better.*

"And?" Michael glanced over to her as they cruised up the motorway heading for Muenster.

"If you like, I'll tell you all about it later, when we eat, we'll have time then, if you don't mind."

"Of course not, it is part of your life, after all."

Well, I wasn't expecting that!" thought Sophie, thankfully.

"Shall I put some music on? I've bought *Silbermond*'s new CD, you like them so much."

"Oh yes, please."

She almost asked him whether he knew Irene Papas, but she definitely belonged in the world containing Corfu and Rolf.

"It is just as warm here, as it is in Greece," she commented as they sat at their table after having placed their order. "In the news they are saying that it is going to be a really hot summer ... well, that's fine with me!"

Michael raised his glass. "Let's drink to your safe return, Sophie ... and again ... you look fantastic!"

"Thank you, Michael. To your health ... to our health."

That was the first time that he smiled.

After their meal, they had enjoyed an excellent salmon dish with summer salad, Michael said: "If you like, you can tell me all about your holiday now, Sophie, I will listen, and I won't interrupt, I promise."

Two hours later Sophie had recounted her story and had omitted nothing.

"And what are you going to do now?"

"What am I going to do now? I am going to lock it away into my memory.

"Then you had better give me the key!" he said, smiling.

Sophie took his hands in hers. "Thank you for that."

"I've just got one more question, Sophie. What would you have done if I hadn't wanted or been able to listen to all of that?"

"Then I would have boarded the next flight."

THE END

Postscript

If you were to visit one of the cited locations, please greet the owner from me. Furthermore, I would be very happy to receive a short message by email at: ascoach@ascoach.de
I hope you have a lovely time on "my" island.

On the website: **www.wie-vor-jahr-und-tag.de** you can find photos of the locations mentioned in the novel as well as pictures of and links to the restaurants and taverns that were visited.

You are also very welcome to send me your favourite photographs of the island, which I can upload to the website. With your permission I will also cite your names with the picure, if you wish. Many thanks!

Best regards,

Klaus Biedermann
Web: www.ascoach.de
Facebook: Dr. phil. Klaus Biedermann
Instagram: dr.phil.klaus_biedermann

The following books and CDs by Dr. phil. Klaus Biedermann are also available:

The Trilogy Tench álin (three volumes)

  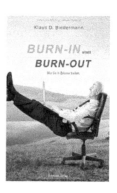

Inway

Mentales Training
Entspannungstraining

Reisen in Trance

Zwei Fantasiereisen
1. Innerer Ratgeber
2. Besser schlafen

Entspannungs- und
Visualierungstraining

Resilienz
Burn-Out Prophylaxe

Zehn Reisen in Trance

und positive Suggestio-
nen für geistige und
Mentale Gesundheit

Lightning Source UK Ltd.
Milton Keynes UK
UKHW011456230620
365452UK00005B/1055